I0670651

ANN
GREYSON

BIRDWATCHER

First Edition: July 2022

ISBN 978-0-578-37615-8
LCCN 2022904890

Printed in the United States of America

I'd like to acknowledge the assistance of my editor, Alexis Miller, founder of the Purple Shelf Club.

BIRDWATCHER

Prologue

2016. Stroudsburg, Pennsylvania

IN THE HEAT of a mid-August day in Pennsylvania the sun hovered over the Pocono Mountains, casting shadows and light through the trees. Ryan Messer, or so he called himself, shielded his eyes from the harsh reflection of the sun as he walked from the parking lot, and slid through the stragglers and into The Stroud Inn's lobby.

When Messer's feet reached the carpet, he paused for a moment to let his eyes take in the room. The posh inn's lobby was decorated with quaint paintings on the paneled walls, high-end furniture, and brown-and-red checked carpeting. The warm, rich smell of fresh yeast dough, garlic, and tomato sauce emanating from the restaurant adjoining the inn drifted through the medium-sized lobby and tempted him. His eyes wandered over to a double set of doors, next to a souvenir gift shop with two large display windows, across the lobby. Over the doors was an old-fashioned sign lettered in gold script: Victoria Station.

The scents distracted his thoughts. But he wasn't a man to be deterred for long from his set course, and he became familiar with his surroundings. He studied the room and its furnishings, and made a mental note of the exits, though there were few. Then he took a quick trip to the bathroom to refresh himself.

The inn's lobby was empty when he returned. Check-in was at 2:00 p.m. Since it was after twelve o'clock, at that moment, little else but lunch was on his mind. He really felt like he could use a good square meal. He'd spent the past few days driving all the way from California, stayed in two-star motels, and ate at fast-food places.

Pushing through the doors, he turned down a short, covered walkway, opened another set of double doors, and stepped into a train car restaurant, a replica of a European railroad dining car. He stood in the corner and took it all in. Its vintage touches of dark mahogany tables, heavy white-linen tablecloths and matching napkins, low lighting and table lamps, red velvet walls, and luggage racks above the tables thoroughly impressed him.

Not a moment sooner, he eyed up the maître d' standing behind the podium in a roped-off area with a pile of menus in his arms. Adding to the nostalgia, he was dressed as a conductor in a black double-breasted suit and a gold-trimmed wide-brimmed hat.

The maître d' noticed him, shot him a glance before asking. "Welcome to Victoria Station. Just one?"

By the tone of his voice, Messer could tell that the maître d' always trotted out his same welcome speech.

He nodded and followed the maître d' to a table, the last one available, next to a table where a silver-haired man in an olive polo shirt untucked over tan Dockers was seated. The man attempted to make eye contact with him as he removed a Korean War-style olive-billed hat with earflaps. Before turning to leave, the maître d' gave Messer a menu, with which he proceeded to cover his face. The man peered at him oddly. Perhaps it was rude, but he didn't want to mingle with any people. Despite the décor and the very touristy customers, he didn't want to be noticed.

After a few minutes, the waitress, Estelle Rowland, came along and flipped her pad.

"Can I start you off with a glass of wine? We have a wide selection of imported wines," Estelle asked him as she absently pulled the pen out of the knot of hair that was piled up on her head and tapped it on the pad.

The sound of her whiny voice jerked Messer right out of his reverie. He didn't like the sound of her voice, not one bit. But he thought it was ironic to hear her say that considering his line of work in the Napa Valley north of San Francisco. His blue eyes moved from the thick strands of hair hanging loose around her narrow neck to her face but not her eyes. He studied her with a less than interested gaze, asked for a roast beef sandwich, French fries, and a Diet Coke, and then his eyes skipped away quickly.

There was just something strange about him, she kept thinking about how he wasn't acting naturally. What was peculiar to her was that he was trying too hard not to look in her eyes.

Without a further thought, she wrote down his order, and disappeared into the kitchen.

A handful of minutes later, all that was left of his sandwich was a smattering of crumbs on his plate. Now, he was polishing off the last of his fries by dragging them through a glob of ketchup. Then he drained his glass and craned his neck around the room, scanning the restaurant for the waitress. When she looked his way, he raised his empty glass as a gesture indicating that he wanted a refill.

Mere seconds after, his eyes fell upon an Amish couple with a young child. They had just sat down at a nearby table. He'd heard about the Amish people in Pennsylvania, but it was his first time seeing Amish people up close. He couldn't help but stare and stare. It took a minute for the woman to notice him, but once she did, she looked at him with apprehension, and then turned back away in her seat. He thought she should be used to people staring at her like that considering she had a bonnet on her head and a simple dress not to mention the man wearing a straw hat, pants pulled high above his waist with black suspenders, and sporting a beard around his chin.

As Estelle cleared away his plate, he asked for the check. He dropped cash on the table to cover the meal and tip, then looked at his watch and rose to his feet, his duffle bag over his right shoulder.

Ryan Messer began walking out of Victoria Station without raising his eyes from the floor. He didn't want to be remembered and tried desperately to disappear from anyone's sight. As luck would have it, his desperation affected his spatial awareness, and he nearly collided into Estelle who was carrying a tray of drinks.

She said, "Oops," caught his arm, set his arm right again.

He smiled at her but said nothing. Then he turned his face away, refusing to meet her eyes and continued on.

Estelle paused, blinking gently behind her glasses, cocked her head and cast a probing glance at him as he walked out of the restaurant. Dark denim jeans, and a two-toned, three-quarter-sleeve baseball shirt. Despite the fact he had a strange vibe, she didn't realize what was walking among her.

Outwardly, he seemed normal enough. That was exactly the way he wanted to look — he wanted to look like a harmless man. And he was able to function normally in society. But he was a psychopath. He might be sitting next to you on a plane, standing behind you in line, and you would never notice him. He could carry on a completely normal conversation with you and a few minutes later, you would not recognize him. Nothing about him stood out. He was just ordinary. That was why nobody would ever suspect him; nobody was going to catch him.

For now, Estelle had plenty of customers to serve in the restaurant and more walking through the entrance. On this busy Saturday afternoon, there wasn't time to think about anything else except her work.

In any case, it wasn't often that Estelle Rowland encountered an odd customer, but this one caught her attention. And that was something Ryan Messer hadn't planned on.

Chapter 1

IN THE four-county region of the Pocono Mountains in northeast Pennsylvania, sat The Stroud Inn, a sturdy old-fashioned elegant five-star accommodation famous for its chateau style of architecture, Romanesque archway, clay Spanish tile roof, and grand fireplaces. In the center of the medium-sized lobby was a massive circular registration desk made of solid oak. Behind it was an office, with a woman in a simple brown dress at a desk.

For nearly ten minutes, he'd been leaning against the counter of the registration desk of The Stroud Inn, watching, taking in the room, making mental notes of things that could be important later. The place was a tad dainty, but it served as a good cover. Well, most of his kind stayed in flea bag motels. *The less conspicuous the better*, he thought, wanting nothing more than to blend in and go as unnoticed as possible.

It was his habit to show up early. He needed to scope out the place for ceiling-mounted pan-and-scan video surveillance cameras, and entrances and exits. Every detail was important. If he was going to get away with something, he had to be one step ahead of even himself. He thrived on risk; the thrill of doing something wrong and getting away with it. It kept him on the edge.

The concierge became aware of his presence, gave him a questioning stare, frowned, came out of her office, and approached him.

"Good afternoon, sir. If I may introduce myself. My name is Ms. Adrienne Weiland, the concierge. Are you waiting to check-in? If you give me your name, I can confirm your reservation," she inquired, trying not to seem suspicious.

Absorbed in his own thoughts, he turned in a startled way. "The name is Ryan Messer. No need to go through the trouble. I called earlier this morning and confirmed my reservation."

Taking him at his word, she responded with a tight smile before she spoke again. "Check-in isn't for another thirty minutes. Perhaps you would like some tea or coffee while you wait?"

The concierge had an understanding look on her face, a face that came from her experience consoling guests, a face that went with the job.

"Now that you mention it," he said, moving in a little closer, "coffee would be great."

Often accompanied with a smile, he tended to lean into females he found attractive, moving into their space, like it or not, welcomed or not. And he was cool enough to look appeasing. At six feet, his brown hair tended to be unruly if he let it grow a fraction too long. He worked out to keep his upper body in shape. But his best feature was his dimpled smile, warm and welcoming, which gave the impression that he was a friendly, outgoing thirty-one-year-old.

The concierge took it all in stride, thinking he was just that kind of guy. *He wasn't ugly*, she thought, *but there was nothing about him that would catch the eye, either*. What she failed to notice at such a proximity was what his victims saw — his dark, bottomless lust, and that deep down, he was too cold.

"Well, welcome to The Stroud Inn," the woman stuck out her hand for a shake, and he reflected that you could hear that capital *S* in the concierge's voice, like you were supposed to hear it.

The Stroud Inn was located on Stroudsmoor Road in Stroudsburg, roughly three miles from the borough of East Stroudsburg. The Lower Brodhead subwatershed that flows for 6.5 miles, marked the boundary between the twin boroughs in Monroe County, the center of the Poconos. The wind moved slowly in the surrounding pine trees, carrying the aroma of fir and sweet-smelling resin. Not far from the inn, discreetly among the trees, were surrounding cabins.

"Glad to be here," he said formally, letting go of her hand almost in the same instant he touched it.

Messer knew he'd better back off, reminding himself why he was there, and wanted to distance himself from her memory. But he didn't worry much about it. He knew that she wouldn't remember him after he was gone. His one blind spot was his tendency to assume that because all his life most people often forgot he had even been around.

The concierge noticing simply lifted her right eyebrow and said nothing. Then she turned away to fetch a cup of coffee.

He was glad she vacated his space but kept his eye on her, watching her scuttle off through the lobby, twice casting backward glances at him. Her blonde hair spilled across the shoulders of her brown dress. *She had a good figure*, he thought, as he openly sized her up.

When he was younger, he didn't have any luck with girls. He remembered when boys in his senior high school class openly bragged about all their sex-capades, hooking up with girls. In turn, he'd just made stuff up, and they believed him. This was in part because of his brown wavy hair and bright blue eyes that were set above a snub nose framed by slanting cheekbones. He was good-looking enough to attract the interest of some friends and dates with the girls, but nothing more. Nor did he care.

"Mr. Messer?" The concierge paused and asked more loudly than she had intended to, "Mr. Messer?"

He jumped, startled by the sudden flash of recollection that he was Mr. Messer. "Sorry. I was daydreaming."

"Here is your coffee," she said plainly.

Messer took the cup from her hand with a simple thank-you and watched her return behind the counter of the registration desk and converse with the clerk. For a quick moment she peered at him, and he nodded coolly at her all the while thinking that by the time he left the inn she wouldn't remember his face.

The muted ding of the silver-plated bell interrupted his thoughts as the clerk on duty struck it, then said, "Next in line please!"

It was now two o'clock. Taking a final sip of coffee as though he wasn't in any hurry, Messer set his empty cup and saucer on a nearby side table. Then he casually stepped behind a young couple and waited for the clerk to get around to him. He had plenty of identification, but nothing in the name of Ryan Messer. Officially, he didn't exist. He'd hide behind that fake identity since law enforcement couldn't connect him to that name. Therefore, he would pay with cash.

He collected the key card and made his way toward the room. In the hallway he angled his head to avoid the video surveillance camera and put on gloves to open the door. The room was decorated in shades of mint, pearl-white, and the palest gray, which made him look pallid in the mirror of the bathroom cabinet.

Things were too quiet for him. Unconsciously, he started whistling, which he often did when he was nervous, while looking around the room. Finally, he dumped his duffle bag onto the bed, then went outside.

Feeling confident that he had parked out of view from the only video surveillance camera that faced the parking lot, he got into his pickup truck and drove off to search for prey, anywhere one might find tourists. He was on the lookout for a specific type. And that was the only reason he was there.

Chapter 2

BEING a well-established mountain resort area, the Poconos, perhaps today was the best-known tourist destination and highland region located in Wayne, Pike, Monroe, and eastern Carbon counties of northeastern Pennsylvania. The series of flat-topped mountains that extended northeast and southwest and linked up with the Catskill Mountains to the northeast was also popular for those seeking the tranquil atmosphere of lakes and nature.

Enter the Wincoffs. A nuclear family, mother, father and one child, that lived in a typical suburban house in a typical mid-American suburb in the Watchung borough in Somerset County, New Jersey.

As his black Buick Enclave SUV crossed the Pennsylvania-New Jersey border at 3:45 in the afternoon, Lance Wincoff continued driving west on the four-lane interstate 80 passing over the Delaware Water Gap Toll

Bridge. Their drive gave a full scenic view of the stunning Delaware Water Gap, a 1,200-foot-deep narrow gorge carved out by the Delaware River through the hard, rocky slabs of the Kittatinny Ridge, or Blue Mountain. Atop the Kittatinny Ridge was the route for the Appalachian Trail.

Lance and Gillian Wincoff felt relieved to pass through the gateway to the Pocono tourist and recreational destinations, to be away from it all, even if it was just for five nights. For Lance it was a break from his often stressful job in real estate and Gillian, a break from her day-to-day running of the household. They would stay at a cozy cabin in the woods, where there was poor cell-phone reception, and no Internet connection.

Her parents, both in their early forties, enjoyed trips to the Poconos before Abby was born but found it to be the perfect vacation for their daughter as well. They would return home a week before Abby's first day of 7th grade. And with the delightful memory of the Poconos trip fresh in her mind, she would have something to share with her friends at school.

Twelve-year-old Abby sat in the backseat of the SUV playing with Carrie, her dark-haired doll dressed in a red polka dot dress. She was quiet most of the drive down into Pennsylvania. But now she was bored and started humming, then singing an off-key rendition of "Little Bunny Foo Foo." In the passenger's seat, her mother had a pleasant expression on her face while listening to her daughter sing. She smiled at her daughter in the rearview mirror, then looked out at the road ahead and saw the sign that said they were ten miles from East Stroudsburg, Pennsylvania.

Abby's mother was an average-looking woman, round-faced, thin-lipped, a chiseled nose, and hair done with a blonde rinse tied back in a ponytail. She had a small mole above her lip, like a beauty mark, a genetic anomaly that Abby shared with her.

In 2016, a day and age where women were more liberated and independent, Gillian found life as a typical suburban stay-at-home mom satisfactory. She didn't have any moral qualms about her role as a stereotypical wife and mother. She simply fell into it after becoming pregnant shortly after her marriage, three months after obtaining an undergraduate degree in English from Rutgers, The State University of New Jersey in New Brunswick.

It was at Rutgers where Lance had gotten his MBA and met his future wife, Gillian Sisler. He was born in the Bronx area of New York, graduated from The Bronx High School of Science, and had gone to New York University for his bachelors. He was a small-framed man of average height. Despite his high cheekbones and a medium-sized chiseled nose, overall, he had a slightly soft appearance. His sandy brown hair had just the right amount of wave in the front, and he was dressed in khaki pants and a white V-neck T-shirt.

For just a second, Lance chanced a sideways glance at his wife. He returned his eyes to the road, driving with his left hand and gesturing with his right.

"Look what's coming up ahead," he cheerfully said.

"We're going through the mountains," her mother said, pointed up the road, then rolled the window down a little to enjoy the mountain air.

Abby stayed quiet several moments, then asked, "How much longer till we reach the cabin?"

She stuck out her lower lip and blew a strand of hair that had escaped from her ponytail and was dangling near her eye. "Probably ten minutes."

Soon enough, East Stroudsburg appeared, followed by a Gulf gas station and a Dunkin' Donuts, then a sign for a Days Inn. Lance Wincoff made a right at a stop sign and went down a road flanked by a patch of pine trees, passing a yellow warning sign featuring a black silhouette drawing of a deer crossing the road.

Her mother glanced in the rearview mirror, saw how Abby was leaning toward the window, a flush of excitement in her cheeks. She knew her daughter was a fan of wildlife observation. In particular, she fancied birds the most and had become an avid birdwatcher since picking up the hobby at age eight from trips to parks during summer breaks from elementary school. Back in Watchung, with wildlife all around them, Abby could tell the difference between a robin and a sparrow. There were few species of bird that she could now see in Watchung that were new to her and therefore she looked forward to spending time spotting potentially new species of birds in Pennsylvania.

Staring at her for a bit longer, her mother could tell her daughter was already planning to birdwatch the minute they arrived there. From the fascinated expression on Abby's face, she could only suspect.

"We're almost there, sweetheart," her mother said with a reassuring smile that prompted Abby to look back at her through the rearview mirror and return her smile.

On this 21st day of the month of August everything seemed right for the Wincoff family. They all looked forward to this summer retreat, expecting to have a great time with no reason to think anything to the contrary.

Chapter 3

THE WINCOFF'S rental cabin was situated in the heart of the Poconos region conveniently near many resorts. Going down the winding Route 209, their SUV veered off onto Milford Rd.

"Take a left," Gillian said anxiously anticipating how close they were to the cabin.

The glorious golden light of the sun flooded down on the red-gold autumn landscape. They were traveling on Sellersville Drive where every so often, a space would open up between the trees, and they'd see a peaceful meadow area for a couple of seconds before the trees closed in again.

A quarter of a mile later, Lance turned the vehicle right. There were more trees packed in on both sides as the Buick surged forward on the backcountry road.

Traveling around the end of a dirt road, the trees parted before them, giving them a view of the chestnut log cabin.

Sunshine cut through the pine trees that sheltered the cabin that wasn't far off the dirt road. On the other side of the cabin, the dirt road picked up again and wound into the woods.

"Whose car is that?" Abby asked of the black Toyota Camry parked by the cabin.

"It's the rental agent's car. She's here to check us in, tell us about the place, and make sure we have all we need," her father told her.

The moment the SUV stopped, Abby unfastened her seat belt and moved toward the door, wanting to birdwatch, that instant. It was as her mother had suspected earlier. Abby had her heart set on spending most of her time on this vacation outside the cabin. It was the only thing on Abby's mind from the get-go.

Before setting off for the Poconos, her parents had explained to Abby that her birdwatching was limited to the trees surrounding the cabin in full view of her parents from the cabin's windows. The woods were off-limits unless accompanied by an adult. And she had agreed to her parents' conditions.

As her hand touched the door handle, her mother turned to face the backseat. "You might want binoculars."

"Hand them to me please," Abby said eagerly.

"You got it," her mother said, and from a compartment in the passenger side of the Buick she retrieved the Zeiss binoculars and handed them over.

Abby slung the binoculars around her neck. "Thank you, Mommy."

"Just remember to stay within view of the windows of the cabin. And no more than forty-five minutes," Gillian said with an affectionate smile.

Right before she opened the door, her hand already on the door handle, her father added firmly. "Stay where we can see you, Abby."

Abby agreed, and her father nodded indicating she could leave.

Without further delay, Abby, her sandy brown hair done in two braids, exited the SUV. She raised her head, squinted, and gazed up at the sky feeling the late-afternoon sun warm her face.

"She loves those birds," Lance threw in as he started to open the driver's side door.

"She sure does," her mother said just as the back door flew open.

Abby climbed into the backseat, where she had left her doll, sitting primly. Her doll went everywhere with her.

"Carrie likes birds too," she said, grabbed the doll, got out and slammed the door.

Gillian and Lance looked at each other, bemused, but said nothing for a moment.

"I'll get the keys from the rental agent, get our things from the trunk and meet you inside," he said, stepping out of the SUV.

She nodded at him but made no effort to leave the car, content to relax and take in the scenery.

Lance Wincoff stood tall, stretched his arms overhead in the very instant that the front door burst open, and the rental agent stepped out.

"Welcome to the Poconos, Mr. Wincoff. 4:30 on the dot. You're a man of your word, right on time," the middle-aged woman said kindly.

Gillian cranked the passenger-seat window down. She relaxed in her seat and watched her daughter through the open window. Outside the door of the cabin, her husband carried on a conversation with the rental agent, who was dressed in neat black slacks and a light yellow, short sleeved summer cardigan.

With her binoculars, Abby, followed the magnificent hawk that soared overhead, the brilliant, shining sun in the background. Her doll was safely tucked under the armpit of her powder blue sundress.

After the quick tour of the cabin, the rental agent handed over the keys and told him everything he could possibly want to know about the cabin before leaving.

"Call me at the office if you have any questions," she said as Lance followed behind her out the door.

Just before opening the door of her sedan, out of the corner of her eye, the rental agent noticed Abby and turned to face her with a cheerful smile.

"Hello there, and what is your name?"

She lowered her binoculars, looked up at her and responded shyly. "Abby Wincoff."

"Well, it's a pleasure to meet you, Abby. My name is Ms. Joy Franklin. But you can call me Joy. If you find anything unsatisfactory with your stay here, you make sure to give old Joy a call," she said graciously.

"I will," Abby said softly, and began fiddling with her binoculars.

"Have a pleasant rest of your day," Ms. Franklin said, entered her car and drove away.

Still sitting in the passenger's seat, Gillian listened to her husband open the trunk of the Buick and retrieve their belongings. For a short moment, she shifted her eyes from her daughter to her husband, watching him carry some of their bags through the front door of the cabin.

Chapter 4

NOT LONG AFTER Lance Wincoff entered the cabin, his wife started unloading the last of the things from the Buick. Awkwardly, she made her way toward the cabin holding a suitcase, along with her shiny white handbag looped over her arm.

"I'm heading inside, Abby," she hollered out to her daughter who was standing just feet away from the SUV looking through her binoculars.

"Okay I'll be right here," Abby answered.

With a degree of effort, she pushed open a wooden door. A musty-smelling, massive cathedral-ceilinged living room, wrinkled her nose. The furniture wasn't new or contemporary, but it was well kept and strategic. The large couch was a neutral shade of beige, matching easily with the curtains that hung around the two windows, and covered in throw pillows that brought color and style to the room.

The oak floor was mostly covered with a black and burgundy Oriental rug. A beautiful old grandfather clock, stood in the corner near the two story-high stone fireplace, its hands moving.

Gillian walked into the bedroom and set her suitcase down on the bed with a sigh of relief. Next, she pushed aside the heavy rose velvet curtains that kept the room in darkness due to the feeble pale light from the ceiling fixture. Then she turned and dropped her handbag on the nightstand and changed her clothes in favor of a pair of faded jeans and a comfortable, pearl-buttoned silk shirt and bundling up the ones she had been wearing.

"I just told Abby that she could stay outside no more than another twenty minutes," Lance said, walking into the room, and stepping to the window to keep an eye on his daughter.

"I'm really glad we're here. And you need this vacation the most. I've noticed how exhausted you were from the long hours you've been putting in at work lately," she said and began to unpack her belongings, placing them in their proper places.

"One of the hazards of being a realtor is that your time is not your own. Must I remind you that the perks include lush vacations like this?" he explained from the window with his back to her.

"I understand all the benefits. But I am very much looking forward to your retirement in twelve years, and the free time you'll have to spend with me and Abby," she said before walking down the short hallway that led to a bathroom at the rear of the cabin.

The room was quiet now, and Lance began to take interest in having some coffee. He found the kitchen, which was an irregular-shaped room with windows on two sides, and a vaulted wood beam ceiling. His brows furrowed when he noticed the automatic coffee maker was installed under the cabinet next to the pantry door. Eyeing his daughter from the window near the kitchen sink, he quickly got the coffee maker going.

The sun was shifting among the leaves in the branches of the trees above Abby in the same moment that the goldfinches perched on the branches took flight in a loud flurry of wings. She turned her head to follow them, the movement almost lethargic, her neck a little stiff from looking up through the binoculars for a long time.

Two chirping goldfinches were perched on a birdhouse shaped like a little red barn hanging from one of the branches of a huge green pine tree outside the living-room window near the cabin's front door. She took a few steps closer, and her gaze shifted to keep a watch on them.

Abby had been outside way past the allotted forty-five minutes. She was still birdwatching instead of unpacking her belongings, which had annoyed her mother. She'd been watching Abby through the living room window.

But a mother needed to have patience. Abby was a child, after all. So, her mother's momentary feeling of annoyance was dissipating. Still, Gillian wanted to tell her to come inside. At the same time, she didn't want to spoil Abby's fun.

Lance appeared behind her, also concerned about Abby. "She's been out there longer than she's supposed to be. Should I go get her?"

"Don't bother. Let's give her a little more time," she said, and kissed him quickly on the lips. "I'll go get her after I get dinner done."

"I'll stay here watching her," he said, took a position at the window.

Almost thirty minutes later, the tantalizing smell of baked chicken and roasted rosemary potatoes and the lingering scent of fresh-baked bread permeated the living room. Gillian set the sleek blond wood table in the dining room and emerged with a full glass of white wine.

"Here you go, honey," she said and handed him the glass. "Let me get Abby."

Gillian called from the open doorway of the cabin. And a second after that, Abby sprinted over to her mother.

"Is it time for dinner?" she asked, and her mother nodded at her.

"Come closer, baby," her mother said, and Abby did.

She put her arms around Abby, who embraced her and held her tightly, as she had been doing ever since she could walk, letting herself be held and rocked awkwardly into her mother's chest.

"I saw so many pretty birds. There's even a birdhouse. Thank you for taking me here."

"I'm happy to hear you say that, Abby. Are you ready for a scrumptious dinner?"

"Oh, yes, mother. I can't wait," she said, drew back, breaking their embrace as her mother put one arm around her shoulders and escorted her into the cabin.

It was a few minutes after six o'clock and yet, the light was fading, eerily. The eager Moon was already out, a thick crescent, sending its light over a cloudless sky. The soft light of the Moon fell on one side of the cabin, the other side cast in shadow.

Chapter 5

MORNING came sooner than expected. Lance Wincoff was not yet fully awake, and the grogginess that came with morning held him in place. Lying in bed beside his wife, aware of the pressure of her thigh against his own, he was struck by how happy he was. He didn't want to get out of bed. Comfortable. Which was part of the problem. Then hunger pangs softly growled, demandingly, in his stomach.

A moment or so later, he slipped quietly out of bed and crossed the hall to Abby's room to check on her. Her head was peeking out from under the cover, and she was still asleep. He thought she looked adorable with her hair tussled. Gently, he ran a finger down her cheek, lifted a stray strand of hair and tucked it behind her ear.

After a smile, he went to the kitchen to make some coffee. As he poured himself a mug of the aromatic brew he had made, he admired the golden rays of the sun that were streaming through the windows sending a beautiful array of colors lighting up the walls. He took a long sip of coffee, inhaling its rich aroma, and letting the caffeine drift into his head.

After setting the mug on the dark granite countertop, he grabbed a box of pancake mix from an overhead cabinet. He pulled eggs and milk from the refrigerator. Afterward, he cracked some eggs into a ceramic bowl with the pancake mix, poured the batter into the frying pan and put the pan on the burner. Saucer-sized cakes immediately began to bubble up. In minutes the kitchen was filled with the sweet scent of blueberry pancakes.

The smell of breakfast drifted into Abby's room, who was up and about now. She came out of the bedroom in her pale-yellow pajamas following the alluring aroma to the kitchen.

After delivering Abby's breakfast, Lance turned back to the six-burner cooktop. Using only one hand, he cracked two eggs at a time into the frying pan. While Abby watched, he flipped the eggs in the air, leaving their yolks perfectly intact. After a few more seconds over the heat, he slid the over-easy eggs onto a plate. Abby laughed at her father's culinary skills in the kitchen, while he shot a sideways glance at her, an amused look on his face. He felt satisfaction at knowing he had impressed her.

Meanwhile in the master bedroom, Abby's mother was awakened by a full-throated chorus of cardinals and northern mockingbirds outside the window. A groan came from her as she started shifting around. She noticed right away that her husband was not in the bed beside her. From the scent filtering through the room, she could tell he was in the kitchen cooking breakfast.

A clock radio sat on the nightstand: the luminous orange numbers said it was 9:09 in the morning.

Gillian stepped in the kitchen and asked her daughter right away, "Abby, do you want to go into town today?"

Just as her husband set down the plates on the round wood table, she fastened her short satin kimono-style robe, with a striped pattern at the sleeves and hem, firmly about her waist over her cotton pajamas. Then she sat down in one of the four ladder-back chairs that encircled the oak kitchen table covered in a burgundy tablecloth.

Abby finished chewing what was in her mouth and just shrugged an okay.

"That's settled then," Lance Wincoff said with bright enthusiasm. "A trip into town it is. After some driving around, taking in the sights and doing some shopping, we'll grab some lunch at Victoria Station in The Stroud Inn. According to our rental agent, it's the finest restaurant in Stroudsburg."

"Dad ... do you mean that nice lady Joy recommended the restaurant?" Abby asked, in a curious tone.

"Yes, she did. She thinks we're going to like it because it's a railroad-themed, steakhouse," he said as he took the last bite of his eggs and wiped his mouth with his napkin.

After breakfast, Abby went to her room to get dressed while her father showered in the bathroom off the kitchen, and her mother rinsed the dishes and put them in the dishwasher.

In the master bath, Gillian brushed her teeth, showered then dressed into a white linen dress touched with stylized brushstrokes of pink. After styling her hair and doing her makeup, she went to her daughter's room to check on her progress. Much to her surprise, Abby was already dressed, and sitting on the edge of the bed moping.

"What's got you down, sweetheart?" she asked softly.

"Nothing. Just thinking," Abby held back.

"I know you want to be outside birdwatching. That's what this is about. You really don't want to go into town, do you?"

Abby looked to the left and nodded her head up and down. "Please don't be upset with me. It's just there are so many pretty birds here. Some I haven't seen before. And with school starting soon, I won't have any more time to birdwatch. So, this is my last chance."

"Don't worry about my feelings. This is your vacation too. After lunch we'll head right back to the cabin so you can birdwatch for an hour or so," she said, and sat on the bed next to her.

With her spirits bolstered, she hugged her mother in a tight embrace. "Oh, Mother, thank you."

Ten minutes worth of driving was about all it took for the Wincoffs to reach Stroudsburg. For some odd reason, Abby was curious about the area. Even she had pushed her doll aside and positioned herself in the backseat to get a better view out the window. She glanced wide-eyed as the

SUV drove through a four-block-long business district passing the post office and big buildings such as the Monroe County Courthouse. Its towering architecture made her feel as though she were viewing it through a giant magnifying glass. And she wasn't thinking about birdwatching either.

Chapter 6

SOON all the sightseeing was over and the Wincoffs were ready for lunch. Abby's father turned the vehicle from Stroudsmoor Road into the parking lot and pulled into an empty space in front of the train-car style building with a sign that read Victoria Station. The popular four-diamond restaurant was connected by a short, roofed walkway to the lobby of The Stroud Inn, a French chateau style red brick building with stone dressings. A top-rated hotel in the Poconos, it sat atop a 350-acre mountain overlooking Pennsylvania and Cherry Valley National Wildlife Refuge, a 30,000-acre wildlife sanctuary.

The door of Victoria Station jerked open before Lance Wincoff could reach for it, and a couple dressed in casual clothes came out walking arm and arm and stopped short at the sight of them. The man stepped to the side and held the door open for the Wincoffs.

"Thank you," Abby's parents said and stepped inside.

As the maître d' seated them, the slim, head waitress, Estelle Rowland was bouncing around the tables. The portion of her thick salt-and-pepper, shoulder-length hair knotted in a pile held in place with a diamond-studded hair stick on the top of her head, and the rest of her hair hanging loose around her neck, made her an odd-looking woman. Though she was dressed very properly in a black skirt, and a white silk blouse with very full sleeves and a white lace dickie.

When her father had said that the rental agent suggested this was the finest restaurant in Stroudsburg, Abby hadn't known what to expect. It was daintily furnished with red velvet walls and had overhead brass luggage racks just like an old-fashioned train car. The linen napkins were in brass-and-silver rings, and the menu had some really rather fancy dishes that sounded delicious to Abby.

Nearby sat Ryan Messer, which was an unfortunate coincidence. He looked to his right, past a muscular man stroking the leg of a woman seated beside him under the table with his foot, an action clearly visible from where he sat, as if he had just seen something exciting.

Messer had just finished his lunch when he caught a glimpse of her. He totally ignored her parents seated at the table across from her. His eyes were immediately drawn to her youthful innocence, literally sparkling in her dress in shades of pink and cream, with short, ruffled sleeves and a double ruffle at the hem. Also, mesmerizing was the little girl's doll sitting on the table, illuminated by the small antique table lamp, its still blue eyes staring straight ahead.

His lips twisted into an ugly grin at the thought that she would be his, all his!

He kept watching her like a cat would its prey, only his hunger was on a different level. And then, the unexpected happened — by another unfortunate coincidence, Estelle Rowland came over, providing an undesired distraction.

"Here's your bill, sir," she said, slapping a little silver tray in front of him.

But Messer just ignored her and eyed Abby, who was fiddling with the straw of her drink.

It wasn't unusual for younger men to ignore a woman past middle age, but Estelle noticed he was gawking at a child. Somehow this alarmed her. Her eyes twinged producing crow's feet at the outer corners.

"Your bill, sir," she said firmly.

Ryan Messer wiped his fingers with a napkin, looked at her. His eyes darkened, studying her oval face, and pointed chin, intently, for longer than he meant to.

They fell silent for a few moments.

She didn't like the way he was looking at her. It felt like he was looking right into her and evoked the same strange feeling she'd felt at their first encounter.

Suddenly, with almost uncontrollable anger he raised his voice and said, "I heard you the first time."

The tone of his voice made several people at other tables look around at them. Astonished, Estelle's mouth opened and shut like a goldfish in a bowl. She glared at him through her black horn-rimmed glasses but had no comeback.

He dropped his voice. "I'll leave the cash for the bill on the table in my own good time."

Messer's eyes flashed just before he went back to ignoring her. He swiveled his head to look toward the little girl's table, which Estelle interpreted as him not caring one way or another. For almost half a minute, she stood in awkward silence with narrowed eyes focused on him as a crow would be on a choice insect. She was highly suspicious, tempered by an intuition that told her he was a shady character. Moreover, there was something about his posture and attitude that she didn't like. And now, as he watched that girl, gazing at her again and again, warning bells jangled inside her mind.

With a sour expression on his face, Messer shifted his attention back to the pesky waitress, leaned forward, close enough she could smell his breath: traces of garlic and some kind of dead animal. "You can scuttle off now."

With a sly smile, he leaned back and thought about how he'd spoken to her — and the more he thought about how he had acted, that she would want to forget him.

If he thought he was intimidating her, he was dead wrong. She faced him with a look of utter disdain. Despite what he believed; his behavior would stay in her mind. She would be watching him closely now. It was arrogant of him to think she wouldn't take notice of him looking at that girl. So much for him wanting to go unnoticed.

"Very well then," Estelle said in a barely audible tone.

With that, she turned toward the kitchen and walked with her head held high. She had to compose herself. She stepped through the kitchen door, took a deep breath, and repositioned her glasses on the bridge of her small, crooked nose.

"I'd really like to kick that guy's butt," Estelle said in a low grumble, inaudible to the chefs and the kitchen crew, and the other waitress that just breezed by her.

Chapter 7

HE waited in his truck drumming his fingers on the steering wheel, his eye on the door of the restaurant. A few moments later he yawned, turned the key in the ignition one notch, the air conditioner blowing out cool air, and he waited. As time stretched, his pulse thudded in his ears, as if quickened by a mounting fear.

After what seemed like eternity to him, the Wincoff family finally made it outside. Messer watched them walk over to their Buick. He followed their SUV at a safe distance. Before long he learned the whereabouts of their cabin. At a reasonable distance from the cabin, he pulled his truck off the dirt road into a clearing — and turned off the ignition. From there he saw the SUV, the family get out, and walk up to the front door, not even noticing him.

He was there less than five minutes.

After starting his truck, Messer shifted into reverse, turned around, and headed back to the road where he had seen a cabin nestled in the trees. After turning left onto Wagon Trail Road, he skidded to a stop in front of a cabin identical to the one the little girl was staying in with her parents. Though this chestnut log cabin was weathered and needed some attention. There was no car in the driveway, and no sign of tire tracks anywhere, suggesting that the cabin was unoccupied. No movement, no sign of life. He knew suddenly that this was where he would hide the shovel, for later use.

He grabbed the shovel he'd stowed in the bed of his truck and made his way down to the side of the cabin. As quickly as he could, Messer pushed the shovel between the wood foundation and the dirt underneath the cabin and returned to his truck.

Before heading back to The Stroud Inn, he decided to stop for gas and a soda. During the drive, he thought again of the little girl. More than anything he wanted to make her his.

Already a plan was in motion.

Ryan Messer prided himself as a man who carefully planned every move he made. Back when he was a kid, he'd carefully thought things through before coming to a decision. Dean, his paternal grandfather, had always called him, his "careful" grandson, and the description had fit him perfectly. Now he was thinking about his father. And he didn't like to think about his father for a number of reasons.

Tomorrow he would start stalking her. He had to act fast because he didn't know how long the family would be here.

But if he didn't get her, he would find another prey, there would always be another, he thought, as he drove on Broad Street and pulled up to the pump at the Valero station.

Forty-five minutes later, he pulled into the parking lot of The Stroud Inn, flung his door open and stepped out of his pickup holding a brown paper bag in his left hand just as Estelle Rowland walked out the door of Victoria Station. The bang of a car door caused her to look in the direction of the sound. The sudden tension in her posture indicated she recognized him right away. Even at the distance of twenty-five feet or so, she could see he was wearing the same blue-and-black buffalo-check flannel shirt with sleeves rolled up to the elbows, faded jeans and big brown hiking boots from earlier. Though she had changed out of her waitress clothes and was now wearing a flowery shirt over her jeans, for a slight moment, she wondered if he would recognize her.

It could be that he ignored her, but she had the feeling he hadn't noticed her. Without glancing left or right, he strode lazily toward the inn's entrance, seemingly absorbed in unwavering thought.

Estelle stopped walking halfway between the entrance to the restaurant and his pickup. She hunched a shoulder. In a smooth and inconspicuous way, she looked at him from the corners of her eyes without turning her head. This way, if he looked her way, she could flick her eyes away and pretend she hadn't been looking at him.

After staring for several seconds, she wondered if the antagonism between them was all but forgotten.

It didn't seem likely, Estelle thought.

Then, for a reason that was inexplicable to her, she could feel a chill creep over her as she saw him open the door and step inside the inn.

Now, she stood alone in the parking lot as an idea came to her — this was her chance to check out his ride.

Right away, she noticed his red Chevrolet Silverado was shabby. For one thing, it was covered with a film of road dust. It looked as if it had been driven across the country, yet its license plates were from the nearby state of Maryland. And the bumper was dented on the passenger's side. *A fender bender*, she thought.

It occurred to her that she didn't know his name and didn't have a way of finding out. She thought on that a moment while she took a quick look over her shoulder just to make sure the man was indeed gone. Thankfully, she didn't see him, or anyone else for that matter.

Just in case, she memorized the license plate number.

Now Estelle was walking toward her black Cadillac DeVille. The four-door sedan was a 2001 and had around 80000 miles, but it was paid off. More importantly, it got her from point A to point B.

She opened the driver's side door, leaned against the car momentarily, and looked back at the man's truck. She had an eerie feeling in her gut, and something told her to get in her car on the off chance of him returning and seeing her. The last thing she wanted was another confrontation with him.

Once inside her vehicle, she popped open the glove compartment, and began rifling through the contents inside. Her fingers made contact with a 7-Eleven napkin. Next, she pulled a pen from her large, black leather handbag with a gold G for Gucci buckle and jotted down the red Silverado's license plate number on the napkin. Then she adjusted her rearview mirror to assure she was leaving the parking lot without detection, before folding the napkin and placing it behind her T.J. Maxx credit card in her wallet.

Five minutes into her drive home, her memory kicked into gear. Feeling a spark of unease pass through her, she remembered the last time she'd memorized a license plate. It had been to help the police investigation of the murder of her ex-husband. When the sheriff came to question her, she told him about the woman in the black Nissan Versa sedan, who she had seen driving him around East Stroudsburg three days before he was found shot to death in his car in the driveway of his house. It just so happened, that on her day off, she saw him in the late afternoon with the woman he was seeing. When her car stopped at a red light at an intersection, she couldn't see her clearly but remembered all but the last two digits of her license plate and the make of the car.

As the investigation progressed, the woman who owned the Nissan Versa, Christal something, was innocent. In the end it turned out that the woman he'd been seeing before

Christal, had a very possessive husband, who in a fit of jealousy shot and killed her ex-husband. So, Christal was off the hook.

With that on her mind, Estelle turned left from Timothy Lake Road. A few minutes before six o'clock, the light of the day was beginning to fade, just as she headed down Allegheny Lane toward the paved driveway of her comfy mobile home that was surrounded by a small plot of grass encircled by tall trees.

Chapter 8

BY THE TIME Estelle parked her car in the designated space at the side of the mobile home and turned off the engine, her thoughts about the suspicious man at the inn's restaurant were long gone from her mind. She used the back of her wrist to swipe a few loose strands of hair back out of her face as she bent her head down to pull out the diamond-studded hair stick. Then she slipped it into her handbag. While it appeared to be nothing more than a simple accessory, it was sharp enough to be used as a weapon if she ever found herself in a life-or-death situation.

When she got out of the Cadillac holding her handbag, she pressed down the button to lock the car door. After stepping out on the ground, she kicked the door shut with her foot and bounded toward the walkway to the porch of her mobile home.

Inside the bedroom of her mobile home, Estelle pulled her work clothes from her handbag and set them on the bed. She went into the living room and picked up the remote from a small built-in table near the kitchen. Then she changed the channel to BRC TV13 out of Lehighton, Pennsylvania, before heading to the bathroom.

When she emerged from the bathroom, the television news was on.

The anchor, Kristi Maratos, an attractive woman in her late twenties with hazel eyes, thick true-blonde hair and a melodious voice bearing a slight Southern accent, began with an incredulous, extra-white toothy grin after the commercial break ended.

"Over the weekend Republican presidential candidate Donald Trump was in Virginia attempting to woo minority voters, asking black Americans to vote for him in the coming election because they have nothing to lose."

Estelle glanced back and forth between the microwave, heating up her dinner, and the TV.

"The more I hear about this Donald Trump fellow, the less I like him. He's some rich old guy, fancy real estate mogul. Just what does he know or even care about the working poor and middle class of this nation?" she scoffed as she tapped her fingers on the kitchen counter.

Something about this Donald Trump had set her off. She slapped the television, then paced back and forth between the kitchen and the living room for a while.

Estelle spoke to the television, pleading with the anchorwoman to move on to local news coverage. But when Kristi Maratos finally did, nearly halfway into the program, Estelle's dinner was almost cold.

Settling down, she sat cater-cornered at the small kitchen table and started to eat.

Talking back to the television set, wasn't unusual for her after living alone many years. This had become her routine and was the activity that she actually looked forward to doing most evenings after work.

There was a good reason she was alone. After being married for what seemed like five minutes in another life, Estelle Rowland wasn't in a hurry to repeat what she considered a mistake. Over the years she dated a couple of guys and found them to be much like her ex-husband. So, she had quit men, at least for the foreseeable future.

Chuck Rowland, Estelle's philandering late husband, had been murdered three weeks after their divorce had been finalized. And of course, his newly pregnant girlfriend, Christal, was the sole beneficiary of his life insurance policy. So, Estelle got nothing. It was a time of desperation — with no money in the bank and no health insurance — she had taken the first job that had been offered to her, as a waitress at Victoria Station. Never in a million years did she think she would still be working there eighteen years later.

For some time, she was upset with herself for not going to college to fulfill her childhood dream of becoming a social worker. And she blamed herself for marrying her husband in the first place. Two months after she graduated from high school, she married Chuck, her high school sweetheart. The sad part was that she simply got married because he was the first one who asked just so she could get out of her parents' house, in order to escape her mother's nagging. Of course, she never bothered telling Chuck that.

Despite it all, Estelle wasn't bitter. Rather, she felt she had had the last laugh. Though it took many years for her to reap the rewards. Sixteen years after Chuck Rowland's death in 1998, his son Alexander with that Christal, had been sent to a juvenile detention facility for dealing marijuana. How embarrassing it must have been for Christal to have a delinquent for a son. Estelle always knew that emotional train wreck of a woman, she deemed a floosy, was not only a homewrecker, but was no good for her ex-husband. And how Christal ended up raising his son was all the proof she needed.

Nowadays, Estelle enjoyed interacting with the public and took pride in the responsibilities that being head waitress brought. In that position, her duties included training new waitresses, preparing the waitresses' work schedules, and relaying requests from the kitchen staff to the waitresses. Her promotion to that position eight years back, was a big help financially, allowing her to enter into an installment sales contract to purchase her mobile home. It was a good-size, single-wide mobile home with a living room in the front, then a kitchen, bath, and two bedrooms, and best of all, paid off two years ago.

It wasn't much, but it was her home, after all.

She had moved from the kitchen to the living room and was sitting in a cream wingback armchair facing the television. Next to her was a huge burnt orange camelback sofa. In her relaxed state, she was in no hurry to prepare for bed. Fortunately, tomorrow was her day off, and she could stay up a little late.

Chapter 9

THE LIGHT from the kitchen window of the Wincoff's cabin gleamed through the trees while overhead a dense bank of clouds shifted from the face of the moon. It wasn't cold, but there was a light summer breeze that had dropped the temperature a few degrees making the air in the cabin cooler.

After leaving the kitchen, Gillian went to the bedroom, changed into her champagne-colored silk pajamas, then tucked her feet into the gold slippers beside the bed. Feeling a little chill, she crossed into the living room, settled onto the couch, and watched her husband start a fire.

Lance dropped two logs into the flames of the fireplace, then grabbed an iron poker from its holder and stoked the fire. He spent the next ten minutes coaxing the flames through the logs to take over the wood. To which they did, sparks popped, and smoke puffed up.

Lance moved across the room and took a seat in a tufted armchair facing his wife on the nearby couch just before their daughter walked into the room. Abby looked around and her gaze stopped at the stone fireplace. A sudden light wind gusted down the chimney, trumping gravity, so that a puff of smoke blew into the room and made the flames dance wildly. For what seemed like a long while, she simply stood there staring into the flames and listening to the slight crackling of logs on the grate.

When she got bored, Abby joined her mother on the couch. Most of the cabin was drafty, but this spot near the fireplace was warm and hard to leave. Abby clutched her doll to her chest and went back to watching the flames while her mother leaned into the couch, getting comfortable.

A lock of hair had fallen across her forehead, and Gillian reached out to push it back. Abby didn't stir. And then her mother looked at the grandfather clock across the couch in the corner. Quarter to ten.

Gillian kissed her daughter's cheek then said softly, "Well, you get on up now, honey. Go kiss your father then get ready for bed."

"Yes, Mommy."

Lance smiled and opened his arms. Abby hurriedly flung herself into her father's embrace, clinging to him tightly without a word. While Gillian looked on and thought it was a special moment, one she would keep in her mind for future reference.

A minute later, she kissed her father's warm cheek, then ripped free of his arms and retrieved her doll from the couch.

Abby waved the doll's arm up and down at him and scrunched up her button nose as she said in a high-pitched voice, "Goodnight, Daddy."

He returned immediately, speaking to the doll. "Sleep tight, okay?"

A wide smile broke across Gillian's face, her bright teeth glowing in the light from the flames in the fireplace.

As soon as Abby walked out of the room, her father left for the kitchen. The moment Abby got to her room, she changed out of her pink and cream dress with short, ruffled sleeves and into her pajamas.

The tree outside the bedroom window rustled in the night breeze, and wood cracked and tore with the sound of a rotten branch breaking off. Curiosity made her go to the window. In the darkness, she couldn't see anything except what was happening in the sky. The moon passed beneath a cloud, lighting it up around the edges. And here and there a star could be seen winking, which was magical to her eyes.

A yawn came over her. She turned from the window and went to bed. Her eyes closed and remarkably, she fell asleep immediately with her doll in her arms.

Lance returned to the living room with two glasses of red wine. He stared at his wife watching the fireplace before handing her a glass. Her ivory skin seemed to glow by the orange light of the fire, and for a moment, she looked like the young girl he'd met and fell in love with long before Abby was born. The one who had a zany sense of humor. The one who had the ability to turn some stressful life event into a joke that could make him laugh even when he knew he shouldn't.

He touched her glass with his, then cozied up with her on the couch. "It's an excellent red. I bought it especially for a special occasion like this."

Leaning closer to him, she took a small sip. "Is this part of your effort to loosen me up?"

His pulse quickened at the undeniable sensuality in her voice and eyes. He drank a little, then set his glass down onto the rustic pine coffee table and watched as Gillian's eyes sparkled.

"What are my chances?" he asked in a sly tone.

"But don't you need your sleep? We're supposed to go canoeing through the rugged beauty of the Kittatinny Mountains after breakfast tomorrow," she answered in a slightly teasing tone.

He leaned close and touched her face. "I know I can get by with a little less sleep."

"In that case, your chances are very good indeed," she said, took the last sip of her wine and placed the glass next to his on the coffee table.

"I was hoping you would say that," he said, slid his arms around her waist, cuddled her close to him and gave her a quick kiss on the lips.

"You sure about that?" she asked, teasing again.

"I'm so certain," he said, moving away from her lips to plant those quick kisses he liked to give under her ear to her jaw line.

Lance held her tightly in his arms and she felt his warmth seeping through the cotton of his shirt. Closing her eyes, Gillian smiled to herself, knowing full well that her life was everything she'd ever wanted.

Chapter 10

WHEN RYAN MESSER awoke the next morning, he stretched himself on the bed. Thoughts of the little girl rolled through his mind. He turned to the digital clock on the bedside table. It was just after eight a.m., time to get moving.

He was dressed and about to leave when a knock on the door startled him. It made him feel as though he'd been caught doing something he shouldn't. Not yet at least.

With extreme caution, he moved to look through the peephole. He saw a man wearing a hotel-staff uniform standing next to a cart filled with dirty dishes, utensils, glasses, and table linens.

"Room service," the man called out. "Pardon me. I've come to collect the dishes."

Messer glanced around sharply, apparently annoyed by the interruption. Another knock sounded on the door. *That was some timing*, he thought as he turned to the low table in front of the suede leather settee by the window where he had left the room-service tray piled with dirty dishes and wadded cloth napkins.

Messer swung the door open, handed the tray to him, then slammed the door shut with a back kick. He stayed by the door an extra moment, scanning the room — trying to recall every move he had made since entering this room — nothing to clean up. As far as he could tell, he hadn't left his fingerprints anywhere. When he had washed his hands, he had used a piece of toilet paper to turn the taps on and off. These little things mattered to him.

As the lock clicked into place behind him, he angled his head to avoid the video surveillance camera and walked down the hallway.

It was a little after ten o'clock when he parked his truck in a small clearing surrounded by trees just off the dirt road leading to the Wincoff's rental cabin. He smiled to himself as thoughts of the girl returned and filled his mind. Whatever her name was. A vivid memory came into his mind of what his life was like when he was about her age. Twelve years old. It wasn't a good time for him.

He remembered it like it was yesterday.

It was recess time on the playground of the elementary school. The kids were lined up facing the captains who were picking sides for a game of kickball. Not a soul was paying him any mind. He was a goofy kid, often ignored by others, that could spend hours on end speaking to himself in a duck's voice. All because he became obsessed with the

1970s tongue-in-cheek novelty song "Disco Duck" by Rick Dees and His Cast of Idiots after hearing it on a Nickelodeon show. None of the kids wanted him on their team. It was no surprise he was the last kid chosen. And, when the captain selected him, everyone on the team shook their heads in disappointment.

Back in those days he was a scrawny kid who couldn't kick a ball, his movements lacking coordination. He blamed his mother, Susannah Rae Dirnberger, for that — she was scrawny too, always dieting.

His mother, God rest her pathetic soul, was born and raised in Easton, Pennsylvania. Susannah wasn't much of a student. Headstrong and irresponsible, she never went to college, and never completed high school. God only knows what she was thinking when she went to work as a receptionist at a YMCA at the age of fifteen. When she was nineteen, she'd hooked up with his father, Wesley Marks, an auto mechanic, and she soon became pregnant. She didn't know if she was happy about the pregnancy herself, but happily quit her job at the YMCA to give birth to him. But then Wesley left her before he was born, claiming he never really loved her and didn't want to be a father at the age of twenty-one.

Soon after he was born, his mother didn't want him. At the time, she was only twenty years old and wasn't ready to face the enormous responsibility of motherhood. And she certainly didn't want to be a single parent. His father's parents were people of means and welcomed him into their home in Fullerton in Orange County, California, and treated him well. Still, his father refused to have anything to do with his upbringing, and just continued working at an auto body shop near the apartment he shared with his friends in Allentown, Pennsylvania.

From time to time his mother telephoned him and sent him presents on his birthdays and at Christmas time. Somewhere in the back of his mind, he hoped she would visit him, even take him back to Pennsylvania with her. But that never came to be.

A month before starting the sixth grade, his mother's communication with him stopped. No more presents.

His grandfather had only told him that his mother had died. Nothing more.

It wasn't but a few weeks after his mother's death that he became a loner. Her death changed him so much so that he kept more to himself than ever before. He was forced to accept that she would never come back for him.

His glazed eyes came into focus. He was back to being twelve years old, sitting in the dugout alone, looking out on the field of the playground. When it was his turn at the plate, he failed to kick the big red ball resulting in an out and preventing a teammate on third base from scoring. Later, in the locker room, he overheard his teammates referring to him as a "blockhead."

That Joey is a blockhead, they said quite loudly.

No one seemed to care if he heard them or not. And many kids laughed at him. He had picked up a dreadful nickname: Blockhead Joey.

One day, shortly after he turned eighteen, he was dealt another blow when his grandfather told him the truth about his mother's death.

"Susannah had gone back to her partying ways. It was on one of her bar-hopping nights that she met a man who told her she could make more money dancing topless two or three nights a week. Much more money than she could at any other job," Dean Marks said, as tactfully as he could manage.

And that, the man gave her the name and location of Classy Lady, a seedy strip joint in Gouldsboro, Pennsylvania. She tried it one night, got lots of cash, and was hooked — spending the next five months dancing around a crescent-shaped stage, gyrating against a pole in a sparkly thong panty — until her murder.

It was the loud cawing of a crow perched on a branch on a nearby tree that brought him back to the present since he had tuned out and gone into his own world. After briefly glancing at the crow, he reached across the passenger seat and opened the glove compartment. He pulled out a roll of black duct tape and a large builder's bag, stuffed them in his black sling bag, then slung the bag over his shoulder. For the most part, his mood was upbeat, feeling like today would be his lucky day, and an unlucky day for his prey.

Chapter 11

OVER BREAKFAST in the cabin Abby's mother said Daddy went into town early that morning to reserve a canoe and get things needed for the fishing trip, which they had planned for later this afternoon. Abby sat at the round wood table, looking terribly bored. On her part, Gillian had completely ignored her daughter's apparent lack of interest. Her mother just carried on conversing adding that she had been up late last night with her father. That she was tired and would take a nap for an hour or so before her father returned. And at which time, if Abby thought she could entertain herself with a pack of playing cards on the dining room table. Abby told her around a mouthful of scrambled eggs that she would do so.

When she had finished eating, Gillian put her dirty dishes in the dishwasher and came back over to her. "When you're done just put the dishes in the dishwasher and I'll run it later."

"I will, Mommy," Abby replied and watched her walk toward the entranceway of the room.

Suddenly she stopped in the doorway, turned, and said, "We're going to have fun today. I promise. We'll paddle the canoe slowly on the Delaware River. And maybe your father will catch some smallmouth bass or trout for our supper. Or maybe you will."

"Okay, Mommy. I'll do my best to try to catch some," she said, sounding genuine.

"And if you see your father before I do, tell him I'm napping in the bedroom," her mother said before exiting the room.

Abby ate the last of her eggs and took a final drink of juice. She carried her plate and glass to the sink, gave them a good rinse, and placed them in the dishwasher. Then she looked around, trying to think of things she could do instead of playing with a deck of cards. But nothing came to mind.

When she walked into her bedroom, her eyes fell on her dark-haired doll. She laid out on the bed to play with Carrie, chattering softly to her. Pretty soon she was humming her current favorite tune, "Little Bunny Foo Foo," to her doll.

At the time Abby was entertaining herself with her doll, her father had just driven into the parking lot of Pocono River Adventures located on Seven Bridge Road in East Stroudsburg. What interested him the most was their advertising of "Old Town" canoes, a nationally known brand of canoes. Since the mid-1960s, the well-known company in Old Town, Maine had been producing fiberglass canoes, but nowadays manufactures most of their canoes out of composites such as Polylink 3, Kevlar, and complex laminates.

Lance went into the rental office and asked the clerk behind the counter about renting a canoe. After listening to the clerk's explanation of their self-guided canoe packages that included all the equipment needed for a canoeing trip, Lance chose the six-mile, two-hour trip down the Delaware River to the Delaware Water Gap, which seemed suitable. For the day's trip, he would pay $104 for him and his wife, and Abby would ride for free because of their special rate for kids. Up to two kids (ages 6-12) rode free with a paying adult.

The clerk, a round-faced, skinny guy in his mid-twenties, reached under the counter and pulled out a map of the area. He opened it up and laid it out on the wooden counter.

After he adjusted his round John Lennon-style glasses, he ran his finger over the map. "This is the spot on the map where the Smithfield Beach canoe launch is on River Road. Right here is where you need to be at one o'clock."

Then the clerk folded up the map and handed it to him. With eager enthusiasm, he continued to explain that the Delaware River pierced the Kittatinny Mountains at the Delaware Water Gap, providing an exceptional view.

With that out of the way, Lance got back in his Buick and headed to the store. He wouldn't be returning to the cabin anytime soon because he had to purchase food, picnic stuff and extra fishing gear.

It wasn't long before Abby was very bored playing with her doll. It should have occurred to her earlier, but maybe this was a good time for her to explore the attic.

With her ever-present doll clutched in her left hand, she snuck up to the attic, quickly raising the stairs behind her. And in that process, she made sure not to rouse her sleeping mother.

There were two light fixtures dangling from the low and slanted ceiling, though the bulbs were missing. For that millisecond a light of almost angelic clarity came into the room. The circular window in the corner was in the direct path of the rays of the sun, which had briefly peeked out from behind the clouds. And she rather liked the eerie atmosphere.

But much to her disappointment, the room was mostly empty except for a rectangular, wooden table and an old television on the top of it near the window.

Abby crept across the creaky floorboards to look out the window. The view from the attic window was like none she had seen. What fascinated her was that the top branches of the trees in the nearby woods were visible. The more she looked the more she thought how much she wanted to be outside.

Right then and there Abby knew for certain what she wanted to do. Birdwatching. That was what she wanted to do. *And that was precisely what she was going to do right now*, she thought. Her mind was so consumed with thoughts of birdwatching that when the doll slipped from her fingers, landing on the floor, she didn't notice.

There was no stopping her. Abby was going outside, unsupervised. When she set her mind to something, she could be as stubborn as a mule — a trait she had inherited from her mother. Even she had left her doll behind in her haste to leave the attic.

Chapter 12

MESSER traveled a dirt path that wound off through oak trees and pine trees to case the cabin. As he moved, he studied the trees. Should anyone see him, he looked like any other tourist. He was dressed in a black and white flannel shirt, with sleeves rolled up to the elbows, black jeans, and brown hiking boots.

Then he stood behind a thick pine tree that afforded some cover, where he had a clear line of sight at the cabin. He leaned on it, and then, with slow deliberation, he ducked down and peeked around the edge of the trunk. He was quick to notice the SUV missing from the driveway. Were they out somewhere?

What was his next move?

His eyes twitched as he considered possibilities. He listened carefully to the sounds of the woods at the rear of the cabin. Among the many birds chirping, he distinctively heard a mourning dove cooing somewhere in the distance.

Just as he was starting to get nervous and wonder if they were gone for good, the door opened, and the little girl spilled out. She wore a thin, short-sleeved, simple white linen dress that showed her dimpled knees. Messer's eyes gleamed with twisted delight as his mind raced with possible strategies, all centered around trying to lure her into the woods.

Abby cheerfully enjoyed the fresh air as she walked to a spot near the trees that was in direct view of the cabin's kitchen window. She wanted to be in plain view on the off chance that her mother should wake up and wonder where she was.

She raised her face to the angry sky as dark, threatening clouds had rushed up over the horizon. A sigh came from her lips. She blinked and lowered her eyes to the ground, disappointment settling over her that there was no sun to brighten the scene.

Within a few seconds she was peering up a tree with her trusty binoculars. She pressed the soft rubber eyepieces of the binoculars to her eyes and adjusted the lenses. Among the branches, she saw a couple of goldfinches chirping happily. How beautiful she thought they were: yellow with a black forehead, black wings with white markings, and white patches both above and beneath the tail. She stood motionless, watching them for quite a while until they all flew away. Then she lowered the binoculars and looked around her.

Ryan Messer was still peeking out from behind the pine tree — a black form in the shadow of the tree that seemed more like a shadow too than a human being. Eyeing her like a poisonous snake, he knew that in order to catch prey successfully, he had to lie in wait, sometimes for hours at a time.

As he watched her placid expression, his hands formed murderous fists at his sides. Messer pictured her lying on the ground, dead. He wanted to strangle her, to feel her life force leap inside him in a bracing jolt — the same jolt he felt from his last kill. All he wanted was to feel that thrill again.

Thinking back to that day, it was a girl about her age. Was that just a coincidence that this girl looked a little like that girl, even though that girl had blonde hair? Yes, it was. But it was difficult to tell that girl's weight from the winter clothes she had been wearing.

A little over a year ago, he was at a resort in the Rocky Mountains of Colorado. In the mountain towns such as Vail, a lot of relatively affluent parents and their children flocked there. He'd had luck tracking that girl. And the snow had worked in his favor. He concealed her body in a snowdrift, sweeping more snow over it and smoothing over the area. Oh, how he remembered so well, all the details fresh in his mind, that he felt a moment's excitement at the thought.

His focus was back on his current prey. He moved a little to his right and peered around the trunk to study her in more detail.

Abby twiddled the string of her binoculars, still looking for a bird. Five minutes had already gone by, and she was beginning to lose interest, wondering if it was going to rain.

For the briefest of moments, she saw the prettiest bird gliding in the sky and watched it land on the highest branch of the same tree she had seen the goldfinches earlier. Staring at the pileated woodpecker with her binoculars, it gently smoothed its feathers. She thought it would make a great pet. If only she could reach high enough to pluck it off the branch.

With a quick movement, the pileated woodpecker was in flight again. Its wings were outstretched, and it was soaring toward the woods. It swooped down and latched onto a tree trunk at the start of the woods. The trees blocked her view, still she could barely see its red-feathered head, watching so intently through the binoculars.

She wanted to get closer to see it fully.

Abby lowered the binoculars and thought about her dilemma carefully. Even though she was enchanted by the bird's beauty, she hesitated as her eyes drifted to the path that disappeared into the woods. She knew better than to wander into the woods alone. Never, ever walk into the woods alone, her mother had told her often enough. The words had been drilled into her mind.

Maybe for a few minutes, she told herself. She couldn't stop thinking about that pretty bird. The canoe ride with her parents scheduled that afternoon was far from her mind. She just stared into the woods, didn't see anyone around, and ironically, felt safe in the peaceful surroundings.

Safely out of sight, Ryan Messer loomed in the shadows behind a tree, thinking she was still in view of the cabin's window. For all he knew, one of her parents could be watching her that very moment. He couldn't take the risk of being seen. No, he reasoned, he could return later.

And his hope that, in time, the girl would venture into the woods had been short-lived. *Fat chance*, he thought, as he was giving up, tired of waiting. Now he was calling it quits. He was about to turn away, keen to be back in his truck when to his good fortune, that was exactly what she was doing, heading toward the woods.

The timing couldn't be any better, he thought.

Chapter 13

IN SILENCE and solitude, and with a sense of wonder, Abby walked into the woods. Even though she knew good and well that she wasn't supposed to do that. But you could chalk that up to adolescence. To Abby, it was like entering a secret world full of whispering trees, with lingering smells of fresh earth teasing her nostrils, all mingled with the warm air.

To any onlooker it was the most innocent sight. A little girl's thoughts concentrated on the sights and sounds of the forest. But the only one watching her was a dangerous predator quite capable of squashing all that was good and pure.

Her parents had warned her about going out into the woods alone, but she just had to see the pileated woodpecker one more time. Caught up in the moment, she wasn't thinking about her parents' warnings.

Undoubtedly, Ryan Messer was hiding behind a tree at the edge of the woods, watching her anxiously. It looked to him like she was tracking a particular bird that caught her fancy. But she had stopped and stood between two oak trees, a spot with a clear view of the cabin. So, he still had to be careful not to be seen. He wondered as he glanced around every so often, why her mother and father hadn't called out to her. As far as he could see her parents were nowhere in sight. Did they even know where she was, what she was doing?

His adrenaline was running high. At that very moment, he could think of nothing other than his need to kill his prey. His cold, soulless stare left little doubt as to what he wanted to do to her. He had to act quickly. Her parents would come for her.

A moment or two later, his head cleared. He carefully shifted himself around the tree and at an angle where he could see her better.

Abby peered through the binoculars at the pileated woodpecker and couldn't take her eyes off it. It scaled two feet of the trunk in three-step hops, probing the bark for food. With a long beak, a tall red crest on its head, long body, and short tail, it was unquestionably the most spectacular of the birds she had seen in the vicinity of the cabin.

"Little Bunny Foo Foo. Hopping through the forest. Scooping up the field mice," Abby sang softly to herself.

The sweet song, the notes all light, for she was a picture of innocence to Messer. His attention remained on her face, noticing that she had perfectly smooth skin. Waiting and watching, he reminded himself to be patient. A flush of temper tinted his cheeks because his patience was running thin.

The branches above her were creaking in the breeze only to be interrupted by the shrill call of the pileated woodpecker. Then it winged noisily away, deeper into the woods. Abby saw the direction it went and wanted to go after it. But first she lowered her binoculars and looked back toward the way she had come from the cabin so she would know her way back.

But it would do no good because she didn't seem able to grasp how easy it was to lose one's way. Especially since her attention span was short because she was too entranced by the woodpecker to really take notice.

As she hurried after the pileated woodpecker, she lost sight of it, then turned in another direction, thinking she saw it. But it wasn't there. It was gone.

Ryan Messer had been stalking her on silent feet — watching her every move. Most important to him was that she had traveled deeper into the woods, completely out of sight from the cabin's windows.

Abby stopped, her gaze sweeping over the area. Where could she be? She turned in a circle, hoping to find a clearing or a road. No luck. Just trees, trees, trees.

Now she was lost.

A strand of hair came loose from her ponytail as she stepped behind a tree, trying to figure out where she came from. The combination of fear and confusion was taking its toll. Which way now? she asked herself. And a little part of her thought, *going into the woods wasn't such a good idea after all.*

Abby was trying to be strong, telling herself not to worry; she wasn't in any danger. But it was hard not to think that when people got lost in the woods there was a chance they could get hurt, or even die. Her body shook a little as she looked to her right, then to her left and back to her right again. She thought about calling out for help. Her mother might be awake and hear her. But in her confused state she assumed that she was too far from the cabin to be heard.

The fear of being lost was rising inside her until a squirrel chippered and scolded from a nearby tree; closer and closer the creature came toward her. She wasn't scared. She faced it down and it scurried off.

Now, she thought about her parents and realized how much she wanted to be with them.

Pausing behind a tree to peer at her, Messer was certain that she was oblivious to the fact that he was there, watching her. There was no doubt in his arrogant mind that he had her right where he wanted her. The element of surprise would be on his side. At this point being calm and alert was the smartest thing he could do. It seemed as if suddenly everything was falling into place. In an inevitable way, it made perfect sense to him. It was a result of all his planning, so that, everything had been leading up to this moment.

"You're making this too easy," he muttered to himself, using a duck's voice.

A pulse was beating in his forehead. His eyes were flashing with anticipation, and a vein was standing out on the side of his neck. The time to make his move was rapidly approaching.

Chapter 14

AT A LITTLE AFTER ELEVEN that morning, Gillian Wincoff woke from her nap feeling well rested. Her eyes brightened just as she came off the bed. She was looking forward to their fishing trip.

But she noticed right away that the cabin was too quiet. That puzzled her. And then there came a strange empty feeling inside her gut when she thought of Abby. She usually heard her daughter clanging around or singing in a soft voice. Right now, her flavor of the month was "Little Bunny Foo Foo." Abby liked to hum it or softly sing some of the lyrics off-key to herself, which was understandable, considering her age. Young children often got stuck on a song they liked and repeated it over and over again until they got bored or found another song, they liked better. And from the quietness, she could tell that her husband had yet to return from his trip into town.

"Abby? Where are you sweetie?" she asked, coming into the hallway.

No response came. Like she was talking to dead air.

"Abby. You there?" she asked, quietly entering Abby's room to check on her.

Abby wasn't there. She turned and walked, fast, to the living room. Didn't find her. Her pulse quickened with each step as she checked the two bathrooms, then the kitchen. But she still couldn't find her. Abby wasn't anywhere in the cabin and when she stepped to the kitchen window, there was no sign of her outside. Something tickled the back of her brain.

Where was Abby? That question ricocheted in her mind.

When Gillian returned to the living room, she paced back and forth to clear her brain. After several rotations, she noticed something she had not seen upon first entering the room: the front door was ever so slightly ajar, indicating the possibility that Abby was outside after all.

Stopping dead in her tracks, she hurried to the window near the cabin's front door. When she looked out, though, she didn't see her anywhere, it finally clicked in with her that Abby was birdwatching somewhere.

The second she stepped out the door, she shouted, "Abby, where are you?"

No answer. Nothing but the chirping of birds.

Without wasting another second, she jogged around to the side of the cabin and called out to her again and again, "Abigail Wincoff!"

Again, there was no answer.

She paused, looked up at the overcast sky, took a deep breath, then turned her gaze to the woods. It was the only place Abby could be. Even though she had a hard time imagining it. She shook her head, not wanting to accept that Abby would disobey her instructions. It was not a certainty, but it was a strong possibility. In the worst-case scenario, she might be lost. But there was no point in her spending any more time analyzing it. She needed to search the woods. She had to find her daughter.

To her frustration, she saw no movement in the woods. She took a step backward, inhaled deeply, and gazed around.

"Abby" she called out tentatively.

Suddenly, a branch cracked off the pine tree to her left. She whirled around. An icy shiver slithered down her spine as she stood there and listened.

For another ten minutes, Gillian was traipsing aimlessly through the woods in a desperate search. But Abby could not be found.

Her ankles ached from rubbing against the hard soles of her Indian moccasin half-boots and she had to stop and lean against a tree to catch her breath. It was all surreal, like she was dreaming. But she was very much awake, and that was the most terrifying of all. In her current state, she didn't know what else she could do except backtrack her way to the cabin in the hope that Abby might be there.

After a moment's indecision, she entered the cabin out of breath, her face was white as a ghost's. A nightmare flood of thoughts raced through her mind in a split-second. Why was this happening? She shouldn't have taken that nap.

"Abby!" she yelled, going back through the cabin, but there was no trace of Abby.

She stood in the open doorway of Abby's room, her eyes bulging with terror. There was nothing to describe what she was feeling in that moment except to say it was pretty downright awful.

"Please, God," she whispered. "Please, God, let her be okay."

Fear flashed in her eyes and her heart thumped sharply. For a brief spell, she stood there gasping for air like a fish pulled from the water. Her face crinkled and tears streamed down her cheeks. Then she caught hold of herself, forced herself to stay calm. She wiped the tears off her face with the sleeve of her white linen blouse, her composure regained but for a vein pulsing in her temple.

Frantically, she rushed to the master bedroom and pulled her cell phone out of her white handbag, waited for a dial tone, and dialed her husband's number. On the fourth ring the call went to voicemail.

As she spoke, her thoughts raced in every direction. "Lance, it's me. Honey, we have a problem. I've been looking all over for Abby, and I can't find her anywhere. I'm so worried. Please hurry back. I'm going to wait ten more minutes, then I'm calling the police. I'm just terribly afraid that…"

A spurt of static disrupted her. Then more static forced her to move the phone from her ear. No sooner did she end the call when something crackled through the static in her mind for just an instant — an engine roared in the driveway then the sound faded away. Her husband had returned.

Turning on her heels, she headed for the cabin's front door. She felt mildly relieved, but her mind was exhausted with worry about her daughter's whereabouts.

Chapter 15

THE FRONT DOOR of the cabin flew open, and Gillian Wincoff called out. "Abby's not here. I don't know where she is."

Lance had his back to her and hadn't heard what she said, while closing and locking the door of the Buick. He turned to see her standing near the door, still wide open, and just stared at her.

"What?" he asked in a casual, off-hand, just wondering sort of way.

"Did you get my voicemail? I can't find Abby!" she said, near to tears.

Suddenly alarmed by what he heard, he rushed to her side and patted her on the shoulder. "I haven't had a chance to check my messages. What is it? What's going on with Abby?"

A sob rose in her throat, and to his horror he watched her blink in a desperate attempt to hold back tears.

"Abby's gone. Lance! Abby's gone."

She tilted her head back. Tears fell anyway. Sorrowful, like rain from her eyes.

A twinge of anxiety rushed through his veins as his mind raced with a host of unthinkable outcomes of this conversation. He opened his lips, but the words caught in his mouth. Nothing came out except his own breath.

He closed his mouth and tried again with a worried look on his face. "Tell me it isn't so, Gillian."

For him, it wasn't sinking in yet; he half hoped Abby would pop up any minute.

"It is so. I'm afraid I have to call the police," she said with a sad sigh, and looked away from him, her mouth trembling, clamping down hard on her emotions.

A choking sadness surrounded his heart. This was sounding bad. But he wasn't ready to accept it. It just couldn't be this bad.

"Please don't report her missing to the police just yet. Give me twenty minutes to look for her. I'll check the cabin and then the woods. If I don't find her, then call them up," he said in a determined voice.

He searched throughout the cabin for Abby, but she was nowhere to be found. With a sigh, he turned around, went outside, and ran around the cabin, looking as far as he could in every direction. No Abby. Then he took off, into the woods. But no matter where he looked, nothing moved but an occasional breeze.

After twenty minutes had passed, he let out a frustrated sigh as he headed back to the cabin to check on his wife, a somber expression on his face.

Gillian was sitting on the couch consumed with worry, her face wet with tears and her eyes puffy from crying. She was suffused with guilt. She blamed herself entirely, wishing she could take back the last two hours, wishing she'd played it differently. If only she hadn't taken that nap. Every minute or so she stopped blaming herself and stared at the door and windows, watching for any sign of movement that might be Abby.

When he entered through the front door, she ran to him, and he grabbed her and held her close. They stayed like that for some moments without speaking, him cradling his shaking arms around her as she buried her face in his chest.

When they separated the silence continued. They stared at each other for an awful minute, neither of them spoke.

Finally, she stated in a matter-of-fact voice that gave no sign of the thoughts and feelings boiling inside her. "I took a nap, believing I could trust her. We talked about this. No going in the woods. She knew that. Abby knew better than to disobey us."

"Is that what you think happened? That she went into the woods," he questioned to make sure.

"Where else could she have gone? She must have gone out to birdwatch in the woods. The binoculars are missing from her room. And her doll is nowhere in sight."

Abby could very well be lost, or something else, something worse. He didn't want to think the worst, but he could not keep the fate of his child from creeping into his thoughts.

"We're wasting time. We need to call the police," he exclaimed sharply.

"I'll call them," she said in a calm voice that sounded eerie even to her.

Immediately she fished her cell phone from her white handbag, lying on the couch. There was one weak bar of reception. She waved the phone above her head, looking for bars. Quickly she dialed 911. The frantic noise of a busy signal punctured the air. She punched in the emergency number two more times, finally heard a bored voice answer on the fourth ring.

"Stroud Area Regional Police Department. What's the nature of your emergency?"

"I need to report a missing child," she said into the phone. "She's twelve years old ..."

"Please hold," the woman's voice was breathy in her ear.

The line clicked and the looped recording of a man talking about Stroud Area Regional Police Department's commitment to serve and protect the people of the communities of Stroud Township, East Stroudsburg borough and Stroudsburg borough crackled in her ear.

Static came on the line. Frustratingly, she ended the call and tossed her phone in her handbag. Besides the bad reception, she knew from experience that here in the Poconos the response to 911 could be slow. Every primal instinct she possessed screamed at her that they needed help finding their daughter now.

Lance walked around the couch and faced her, staring, uncomprehending. "Why did you hang up?"

"I stayed on hold for seven minutes until I heard static. The reception isn't great out here. Anyway, it takes three times that long to drive to the Monroe County Courthouse in Stroudsburg. We passed it on our way to Victoria Station. I'm going there because that's where the sheriff's office is. I want you to stay here. Somebody's got to be here in case Abby comes back," she said, throwing her handbag over her shoulder and walking toward the door.

"Are you sure you're okay to drive?" Lance asked, following her to the door.

"Not really, but I have to. I was here when Abby disappeared and can give a full account of today's events," she said, before slamming the door behind her.

"We'll get through this," he said to the empty room in a comforting voice.

In the kitchen, Lance busied himself, pouring coffee into a mug, reaching into the refrigerator for milk. Then he turned to one of the windows and watched for Abby, waiting for a sign of hope, something, anything.

As he sipped his coffee, he wondered how long Abby had been missing. His watch told him it was three minutes after twelve. A million questions tore through his mind at once. Would she come back at all? Was it too soon to consider her a missing person? Would the police find her? Had he lost her for good?

It took a moment for him to realize that he was losing it a little. Or something close to that. His mind was in disarray. So, he decided to wait outside the cabin. That way he could keep an eye on the woods, looking for any signs of Abby. What else could a distraught man do?

Chapter 16

HIS REAL NAME was Joey Marks, but nobody had known that. No one knew who he was, no one would ever know what he did. At least he believed that.

It was just after twelve noon and Marks was walking quickly toward his Silverado parked in a small clearing. Pausing for a breather, he stopped at the back of the truck and admired the Maryland license plate he had stolen. He was smart enough to steal it from a pickup truck with a similar make to his truck that was parked in a long-term parking lot at the Baltimore/Washington International Marshall Airport. He knew it would be days, weeks, before the theft would be reported. And it was harder to spot a license plate than a stolen vehicle. That was the beauty of it. By then he would be long gone from the area with his California license plates back on his truck.

Then he looked up. He just noticed the buildup of clouds on the horizon, looking like a storm might break at any moment — he hoped sooner rather than later. He smiled thinking that the rain would wash away footprints, blood, and fibers.

With a renewed sense of energy, he got into his pickup and grabbed his Baltimore Orioles baseball cap on the passenger's seat and put it on. It was a souvenir he had bought in an effort to blend in at the BWI Marshall Airport. He pressed the orange-black baseball cap low onto his head. Right now, he wanted to vanish.

He whistled and congratulated himself as he came onto Sellersville Drive. Lost in his exuberance, patting himself on the back, he turned his head a little, and in so doing he lost sight of the road for a second, veering across the double yellow line into the opposite lane.

A honking horn startled him out of his musings. But before he could steer out of the opposite lane, a white Toyota Camry Solara coming toward him swerved onto the shoulder, the car crunching to a gravel halt. While the driver, an older light-skinned black woman, seemed to be cursing, his response was a mere glance in his rearview mirror. Then he immediately turned his eyes forward and chuckled to himself thinking how lucky he'd been to avoid a collision.

His tension drained away when he arrived at The Stroud Inn at twenty minutes after twelve. He liked the sound of the door clicking shut behind him. It meant safety, tucked away in the room. Nobody had seen him. He had gotten away with it.

The first thing he did was go to the bedroom where he reached into the drawer of the bedside table and pulled out the room service menu. Lunch. After all he'd worked up a vigorous appetite and decided to treat himself. He dialed room service, ordered a filet mignon, garlic mashed potatoes, raspberry cheesecake for dessert and two cold bottles of Budweiser beer to wash it all down.

"Will there be anything else?" he asked, mimicking the room service operator with a duck's voice.

As he stared at the silent phone in its cradle, he was amused by the way that the room service people never said anything but "No problem, sir. Will there be anything else" and "Very good, Mr. Messer." And the fact that he wouldn't have to pretend to be Ryan Messer for much longer.

Now he needed a quick shower. He took off all his clothes and placed them into a brown paper bag, which he planned to drop in the trash receptacle of a gas station. He ducked into the shower and turned it on. The stinging blast felt great. He rested a hand on the tile wall and stood there calm while the hot water beat down on him. That was when he felt the hot water wash her away as thoughts of the little girl popped into his mind.

When he came out of the bathroom, wearing only a towel around his waist, he quickly found a pair of navy sweatpants and a T-shirt to throw on. Afterward, feeling refreshed, he planned to spend the rest of the day and part of the evening replaying the memories of the day's events in his mind. And, in the morning, after checking out, he would drive to California back to his work in a winery in the Napa Valley at the northeastern tip of the San Francisco Bay. It was an easy job, sometimes physically demanding, and very anonymous.

In the half-light of the room, he settled onto the bed. Within a minute of laying his head on the pillow with his hands clasped behind his head, he knew he was going to sleep better this night than he had in weeks. Not only had the killing calmed him and gave him peace, but it also gave him a thrill, feeling like a kid on a ride at Disneyland — not realizing much of what he considered "fun" was psychopathic.

His thoughts went back to his first kill in the forest of the Great Smoky Mountains National Park in Gatlinburg, Tennessee, around six years ago. There were others after her, but this one haunted him on occasion and for a very simple reason: He knew he'd been seen. Still, to this day he believed that the witness was mentally challenged and therefore didn't realize what he had seen nor bothered to report it. At least so far. He had even made eye contact with the young black man lingering in the forest. Still, he felt taking his first life was very thrilling for him, despite being seen.

His growling stomach brought him out of his reminiscing. A film of perspiration had broken out on his brow, and he wiped it away with a napkin from the bedside table. To settle his nerves, he spent the next minute reminding himself that he was safe.

He glanced at the digital clock on the bedside table. It was still early for the room-service delivery, but he was counting in his head the last of the twenty minutes for it to arrive. And in doing so, it made him realize just how hungry he really was.

Chapter 17

THE MONROE COUNTY Sheriff's Department was in a three-story, white-limestone building designed by an architect in a fashionable Richardsonian Romanesque style. Built in 1890, the Monroe County Courthouse was on Monroe Street in Stroudsburg's downtown area.

In her frazzled state, Gillian Wincoff passed the turn for Monroe Street on her left and carried on down 6th Street, turned left on Sarah Street, then made a left onto 7th Street to intersect Monroe Street. A cluster of police vehicles sat in a parking lot behind the courthouse, and she wheeled into a visitor's space beside them. The time was now 12:27 p.m.

Inside the courthouse, Sheriff Andy Kirkman emerged from the squad room with a white mug bearing the green logo of the Philadelphia Eagles filled to the brim with coffee. With a nod and a word of greeting to a deputy that wandered past him, the sheriff walked to his corner office overlooking the parking lot. The walls were hung with two plaques, a boxed Philadelphia Eagles jersey, a bachelor's degree certificate from Temple University, and some curling DARE antidrug posters. He unbuttoned his shirt collar and settled into his lumpy black leather chair that seemed to swallow his whole body.

Andy Kirkman was a broad-shouldered man, five feet eight inches and one hundred and seventy pounds. His dark blond hair was cut businessman-short and neatly combed, with a part. Although he was forty-four, he looked nearer to fifty. Given his carefree smile, he had a youthful glow about him. But he had the angular face of a man who'd grown up too fast stemming from his nearly twenty years on the force.

The stack of papers on his cluttered desk seemed to grow every day. But he zeroed in on the coffee that steamed in front of him. Eagerly, he took a sip, which tasted even better than it smelled, took another sip, and sighed with pleasure.

The sheriff swiveled in his chair, the leather groaning with the movement, and powered on the computer and waited for it to boot up. Once it did, it beeped, telling him that an e-mail had arrived. He raised his mug to his lips, swallowed some coffee and peered at the screen. His e-mail program was open. There were two e-mails in the lineup, one unread. Nothing important. He hit a button on the keyboard and closed the e-mail program.

Kirkman scooted to the edge of the bookcase, his chair's casters squeaking shrilly. He grabbed a case file from the top shelf and slapped it on his desk.

The front door of the courthouse popped open a minute later, and Gillian Wincoff stepped inside just as two deputies emerged through a door at the far end of the lobby.

"Ma'am, I'm Deputy Shipley and he's Chief Deputy Livengood. How can we help you?" asked the shorter of the two men, with green eyes and a motorcycle cop's mustache.

Her jaw worked, nothing coming out as she glanced at the two men with their shiny deputy's badges on their shirts, until she asked, "Would you please take me to the sheriff? This is urgent."

The sound of her voice brought the sheriff out of his reverie. He looked up from his notes on his most recently solved case — a 19-year-old cold case murder of a thirty-two-year-old woman who went by the name of Randee Rae Devereux and worked as a topless dancer at the now closed Classy Lady strip joint in Gouldsboro.

"Follow me," Deputy Shipley said, pointing with his chin.

Chief Deputy Aubrey Livengood stood stationary, stifling a yawn. He was twenty-nine, fit, tall, and had a scar that bisected his left eyebrow in a hairless dividing line.

Gillian followed Deputy Shipley, who moved with sure feet, to a modest office done in cherry wood with a cherry wooden desk, off-white walls, and dark gray carpet. The air in the room was cool and smelled like paper, dry, and slightly musty. A built-in bookcase dominated the center of an interior wall and was stuffed with file boxes, and doodads. The metal wastebasket was full.

"I'm the sheriff," he said, putting the pen he'd been twirling between his fingers back in its holder and standing up. "What can I do to help you, ma'am?"

Deputy Shipley hooked his thumbs into his duty belt, which looked like a habitual gesture, before returning to the front room.

She stood directly in front of his desk and stared at him with a desperate expression. "I just don't understand how my daughter could just disappear."

"Are you saying your daughter is missing?"

"Well, of course she's missing. That's why I'm here. My husband and I searched the whole cabin and the nearby woods. She's been …"

"Her name is?" he cut in, coldly.

"Abigail Wincoff, nickname Abby," she said, tears building up in her eyes. "I was taking a nap at the time she went missing."

That explanation was received with a raised eyebrow, which she ignored.

"What time did you take your nap?"

Her mind drew a blank, but then she consciously tried to remember. And in the meantime, he didn't say anything.

"Oh, I remember now. At 9:40, just after breakfast."

"What time did you notice her missing?"

"It was three minutes after eleven when I woke up. I immediately started looking for her around the cabin."

Kirkman nodded, took notes, and asked more questions. In the process she became frustrated.

"Can we do this later today? Time is wasting! You need to get people out and do a search," she finished loudly.

Sheriff Kirkman allowed a moment for her blood to cool and for him to yield to her request. He took a business card from his desk and wrote something on the back.

"My mobile, and my office details on the front," he said, handing the card to her.

She nodded and stared at the plain white card with a raised Monroe County Sheriff's Office logo and gloss black ink reading: *Sheriff Andy Kirkman.*

"As of now," he grunted, closed the case file on his desk, and interrupted, "Abigail Wincoff is my full-time assignment. My other cases have been parceled out."

Shaking her head in relief, she blew out a frustrated huff, and her eyes welled up. A tear trickled from her eye down her cheek, past the black mole above her lip and dripped off her chin. She sniffed and moved away from the desk.

"I gather you're on vacation here?" he asked somberly.

Gillian gathered her strength. "Yeah, from Watchung, New Jersey."

He opened his desk drawer. "All right then. I'll need a little more information, though."

Kirkman selected two forms from a drawer. He shoved them across the desk to her.

"Can you fill those out for me?"

As she made a meticulous account of what Abby had worn, he said in a reassuring voice, "There's a chance your daughter is lost somewhere in the woods, much farther out than the area you searched. It happens sometimes."

She grasped at the slim chance with heartbreaking eagerness. Her eyes were suddenly gleaming with hope.

After asking for her daughter's school picture, the sheriff punched numbers on the base of his fancy black telephone. As soon as someone answered, he gave rapid-fire orders into the phone.

Then, he ended with, "Let's get over there with the cavalry and do a thorough search for this little girl."

Chapter 18

A WHITE Toyota Camry Solara drove down Sellersville Drive in East Stroudsburg and turned right onto Wagon Trail Road, arriving moments later at a beautiful, secluded cabin. The occupant of the vehicle, Millie Dozier, was there to spiffy up the place for the next guest, though her mood was unsettled. She was still shaken up from the earlier incident on Sellersville Drive. That red truck. Well, she did not like him — he was a careless driver, whoever he was. Just thinking about it made her crossed eyes shift like a reptile's.

The fifty-six-year-old black Creole was born poor in the small southern Louisiana bayou town of Plaquemine, some eighty miles upriver from New Orleans. Raised speaking French, Creole, and English, she lived there till she got married and followed her husband to Stroudsburg when he got a job in the hotel industry. Though she moved to the area twenty-eight years ago, she still had a hint of a Creole accent that gave her delivery a slight drawl. But her most distinctive feature was her crossed eyes, which made her awkward.

After a shaky breath, she leaned her head against the steering wheel to calm herself.

Gradually, she managed to bring her nerves under control and forced herself to think about her job. She raised her head, looked straight at the cabin and she saw the curtain in the window move. As she watched, waiting several tense moments for the curtain to move again, loud cawing sounds erupted somewhere in the sky. She looked up and saw three black crows circling above the cabin, and a dozen crows flew out of the trees, croaking in alarm.

When she looked back to the window, apprehension had clouded her face. Suddenly, she felt a cold tingle at the base of her spine. Only half her mind was on her work. The other half was thinking someone was watching her, yet no one was there that she could see.

The electronic chirp of the cell phone in her handbag startled her. She answered the call, listened for a moment, then clicked off. The manager of her cleaning agency, Clean As A Whistle, had called to check on her.

She took a couple of short, quick breaths to clear any foolish notions from her head, telling herself that there was nothing to be nervous about. She'd cleaned that cabin before.

Although she arrived early for her shift, she stepped out of her car and started walking down the driveway. With her right hand she reached into her handbag and found the keys to the cabin. As she approached the door, she heard what sounded like a child's voice singing.

"Little Bunny Foo Foo. Hopping through the forest."

She moved closer to the door so she could hear a little more clearly. But the singing had stopped abruptly. Pausing, she held her position, listening until she heard the voice again.

"Help me," a voice said softly, yet so faint and fleeting that Millie couldn't be sure what it was.

No matter — she froze on account of it, not daring to move another step. Her eyelids were twitching. Then, out of nowhere, a gust of wind rushed at her, carrying a dank odor of mildew. The keys slipped from her fingers and hit the ground with a jangle. She bent down to pick them up and noticed tiny pieces of glass lying on the ground.

Pulling her body back to an upright position, she could see that two of the panes in the window nearest the door were broken. For such a popular tourist area, she knew from prior experience that cabin break-ins weren't unusual. Slowly her crossed eyes moved around, searching for any indication of movement, fearing that the intruder might still be in the cabin.

Not sensing anyone nearby, she hurried down the driveway and got back into her car. Surely, now she would drive away, but she decided at the last possible second to report the incident to the police. They needed to be aware that there were burglars about. For now, she set aside the voices she had heard earlier.

"Today has been the strangest day," she whispered to herself as she pulled her cell phone out of her handbag and punched in 911.

When the 911 operator picked up, she said, "Stroud Area Regional Police Department. Please state your name and the nature of the emergency."

"My name is Millie Dozier. I'd like to report a break-in at a cabin over here on Wagon Trail Road," she said in her slow, French — accented Creole drawl.

"Is the intruder still in the cabin?"

"Not that I know of," she retorted, "but I can't say for sure on that."

"I need you to clearly state your exact address for me."

After Millie gave her exact location, the dispatcher then clearly advised her that the police would arrive in minutes. Furthermore, the dispatcher asked her to stay in her vehicle and close to the phone. And that an officer would come to take a statement from her.

As soon as the call ended, she dialed her work number. She found herself being patched through to her manager's voicemail service and left a message explaining what had happened.

She put the phone away and shifted in the driver's seat, trying to get comfortable. Shaded by the overhang of trees, Millie now turned her attention to the cabin, and fear grew within her. She had a strange look in her eyes, like she was in a trance. And her mouth hung slightly agape as she continued to stare at the cabin.

Very softly, half unconsciously, she began singing. "Little Bunny Foo Foo. I don't want to see you. Scooping up the field mice. And bopping them on the head."

Suddenly, her eyes blinked rapidly and focused. They widened in alarm as she snapped out of her trance. She gasped, then put her hand to her mouth in astonishment.

"What in the world?" she asked herself quietly.

Chapter 19

AT A QUARTER TO ONE, the police began searching the woodland near the Wincoff's cabin while a news chopper was circling overhead. The very thing all parents had nightmares about — a child gone missing. This was something the police took seriously, so they were going to look hard for Abby.

What made matters worse, as if anything could make matters worse, heavy banks of clouds hung low, threatening to open up and make a mess of things. So, with rain showers on the horizon, it wasn't a good day to search the woods for a missing child, but there were no good days for it anyway.

When Sheriff Andy Kirkman pulled into the driveway of the cabin, Gillian Wincoff drove in behind him. The first thing Kirkman noticed was Gillian's hands clasped to her face walking from the Buick to the doorway of the cabin where her husband stood. That image stuck with him: it was pure dread.

On the contrary, Abby's father was driven into action. The moment he saw Sheriff Kirkman walking away from his Ford Expedition SUV, he stormed out of the doorway and approached Kirkman wanting to know details on how the search was being conducted. He even wanted to help with the search for his daughter. But the sheriff thought it would be best for him to stay in the cabin, and let the police handle it from here.

"This is absurd! Abby is my daughter. I can't just sit here and do nothing," Lance Wincoff said with an edge in his tone which cut across everyone's consciousness.

The sheriff crossed his arms over his chest and glared at Lance until he looked away. Kirkman took in every word and then started to say something but changed his mind at the last second.

Chief Deputy Aubrey Livengood rushed to intervene. "I know it's a tough call, especially given the circumstances, but it's best you stay in the cabin and let us do our job."

Livengood had always been a slow talker, known for a long-drawn-out delivery. This time his words toppled over themselves in their eagerness to disassociate themselves from his mouth.

Lance relented with a sigh. "Look, my daughter could be anywhere out there. Just find her. Tell everyone on that radio of yours, there is a missing twelve-year-old. And she answers to the name Abby."

The words hung in the air for a long moment. Then Lance turned on his heel and returned to the doorway to comfort his wife, who was sobbing quietly into her cupped hands. Livengood watched as he threw an arm over her shoulder and drew her in close. Obviously, Abby's father was keeping it together for his wife. The Wincoffs stood silently in the doorway for a moment or two longer, then went into the cabin.

Livengood watched them slam the door behind them. He pitied the Wincoffs, perhaps a little emotion had crept in, but what more could he do? His duty was to follow proper police procedures.

The Chief Deputy turned to Sheriff Kirkman and asked quickly, "What do you make of the scene?"

"I just got here. I can't solve it in the blink of an eye, you know," the sheriff said in an affable tone.

Abruptly, the door of the cabin opened again, and Lance came out. He walked to his SUV, opened the trunk, and took out some shopping bags. Without even looking at the sheriff or anyone else, he slammed the trunk shut and walked back to the cabin carrying the bags. Once again, the door was slammed behind him.

Not a moment too soon, the sheriff started shouting orders to the deputies, hustling everyone about. Kirkman was determined to get to the bottom of this missing child situation. In cases like this, time was of the essence. The longer the stretch of time, the more difficult it was to find the child.

"Give me a shout if you find anything. And I mean anything," the sheriff said, tension in his voice.

With long impatient strides, the sheriff walked through the woods. There was a note of worry mixed with determination in his eyes. This would be his last case and there was nothing more that he wanted than to crack it fast and snag a hefty retirement bonus. Following behind him were his chief deputy and two other deputies, carrying cameras, and other equipment.

It hadn't been but a couple of minutes before the sheriff stopped to examine his surroundings and jotted something down. Whereas, Livengood had stalked off somewhere.

A blast of voice and static came over the sheriff's two-way radio. "Sheriff Kirkman? You there?"

Kimberly Kaasa, the police department's new secretary and dispatcher, sounded impatient and a little nervous.

He plucked his radio from his belt and pushed the talk button, "This is the sheriff. Go ahead, Kimberly!"

The band briefly filled with static, then Kimberly said, "We've gotten a call about a break-in at the cabin out on Wagon Trail Road off of Sellersville Drive, no more than twenty-five yards from your location."

The sheriff waved his hand at Deputy Missy Sparks. She stepped near him, a question on her face. With wide blue eyes, a pale, freckled face and bobbed black hair, Deputy Sparks was twenty-seven, five foot five and had a slim boyish figure.

Kirkman gave a "just-a-moment finger" to Sparks as he listened to the dispatcher on the radio. "A woman named

Millie Dozier, reported the break-in, and is sitting in her car in the driveway of the cabin."

"I'll head over there," Sheriff Kirkman said, then clipped the radio back onto his belt.

"I got a report of a break-in at the nearby cabin. Grab Deputy Shipley and let's head over there," Kirkman said to Sparks, pointing at an angle through the tangle of forest.

No sooner did Deputy Sparks show up with Deputy Shipley than Sheriff Kirkman called out, "Chief Deputy Livengood, Shipley and Sparks are coming with me. Get some more deputies here. And bring in the K9 unit."

After a quick nod to the sheriff, Livengood turned in another direction, the radio on his belt squawking to life as he walked.

Sheriff Kirkman looked at Sparks and Shipley while jerking a thumb toward the dirt road. "Follow me, please."

Chapter 20

MOVING at a blistering pace on foot, Sheriff Kirkman concentrated on their surroundings. The two deputies were doing the same. Maybe five minutes later, they rounded a bend on Wagon Trail Road and the trees opened up to reveal a cabin, which had all the signs of being deserted. The windows were covered with curtains and there was a peculiar silence, like time had stopped. No noise. Even the birds had ceased to chirp.

The deputies walked up to the front of the cabin to wait. And Sheriff Kirkman walked to the Toyota parked in the driveway, quickening his pace as he drew nearer.

A knock on the glass made Millie Dozier jump in her seat. For reasons she didn't understand, she had been dozing off, like her mind was asleep and her body was awake. A man in a sheriff's uniform stood outside.

"Ms. Dozier, I'm Sheriff Andy Kirkman of the Monroe County Sheriff's Department. I'd like to talk to you for a bit."

Wake up, she told herself as she turned the key without turning on the ignition and lowered the window. She answered some questions, then handed the sheriff the keys to the cabin.

Of course, she didn't tell him about the strange voices. She didn't want him to think she was crazy. Anyway, it didn't matter anymore. She had already convinced herself that her mind was tired and was playing tricks on her.

"Stay in the car. Either myself or one of my deputies will come to take your statement, then you'll be free to go," he instructed her.

"I can't just leave! I have to prepare the cabin for guests arriving tomorrow," Millie said, in an insistent tone, her crossed eyes bobbing up and down.

"Not going to happen today," he said before walking away.

After a loud sigh, Millie rolled up the window and sat back against her seat, her arms crossed in front of her.

The deputies were examining the broken window when the sheriff came up to them. Both were already wearing latex gloves, and Shipley passed a pair to Kirkman, who nodded to him as they moved to the front door.

"Let's get to it," Sheriff Kirkman said, handing Sparks the keys.

The sheriff knocked hard on the door. "Monroe County Sheriff's Department. Open the door."

There was no response from within, but Sparks stood to one side as she inserted the key. Slowly she turned the knob, unlocking it. And Shipley kicked the door open, placing his hand on his Glock but leaving it holstered as he stepped forward and went through first.

While Shipley stopped to listen, Kirkman stepped into the doorway. The interior of the cabin was a little dark and cool, and apparently empty. He waved for Kirkman and Sparks to come in.

What sounded like a child's voice, so soft and low, echoed through the ventilation ducts. Simultaneously a buzzing bee dive-bombed the sheriff's ear, like there was a big bull's-eye painted on it, distracting him completely. After swatting it away, Kirkman watched it fly through the living room in front of him, disappearing around the corner into the hallway. Sparks was the last to walk in and simply made a face from the strange, mildew odor that lingered in the air.

"Did you all hear that?" Shipley asked, looking around the living room before stopping on the sheriff.

Kirkman looked at him like, *What?* And Sparks just kind of shrugged her shoulders like she had no idea what he was talking about.

"The place is rather tidy," noted Sparks, changing the subject, and gazing around.

The sheriff instructed his deputies to search every room, every closet of the cabin. They approached this break-in with the utmost gravity because the odds were sky-high that this was connected to their missing child investigation.

In the interim Millie Dozier was still waiting in her car, slouched over in the seat, and talking to her boss on her cell phone. The head of the Clean As A Whistle agency didn't like what she was hearing, especially knowing she'd have to notify the owner of the cabin.

After ending the call, Millie turned her face away from the cabin, which spooked her so much. But soon a movement at the door caught her eye and made her look. She saw Deputy Sparks come out of the cabin, followed by Sheriff Kirkman. Noticing Sparks was walking toward her car, she gave a sigh of relief and sat upright in her seat.

Kirkman looked up at the clouds gliding over his head, so low it felt as if he could reach out and touch them. Then he glanced back at the cabin just as Deputy Shipley was coming out. But in that moment, the sheriff was staring at the cabin with a faraway look in his eyes, deep in contemplation without truly paying attention to other people. Sometimes the sheriff got that look when he was talking to himself inside his head. Then Kirkman slowly turned in a circle, studying the forest.

Stopping a few feet outside the door, Shipley smacked the side of his head with the palm of his hand. He simply couldn't fathom why he'd heard a whispering voice repeating, "help me." *The job was getting to him*, he thought.

Sparks appeared next to the driver's door of Millie's car and looked at the sheriff, his mind entirely on the case. He was examining a dirt path that veered off to the left before disappearing around a bend into the trees. She was sure going to miss him when he retired. In the four years she'd been on the force, she'd seen that he was a hard-nosed realist. That he would act objectively and reasonably, in the best interests of the investigation. Yet he was a kind of jovial, generous pillar in their community, and she, in turn, respected him for all that.

Sparks leaned down, peering at Millie in the driver's seat and tapped on the window. "Would you mind stepping out of your car?"

Deputy Shipley walked over to the sheriff and waited for instructions. He couldn't help feeling disappointed. If a clue was there in the cabin, he missed it.

"If we could nail down this missing child case in a day or two, that would make me a happy man," the sheriff said in a low voice.

"I wish the same, sir," Shipley said, and hitched his duty belt up, then smoothed out his shirt.

Despite not having found anything out of place, that they could tell, the sheriff wanted the cabin dusted for prints and DNA.

The sheriff reached for his two-way radio. Three harsh clicks followed by a slight buzz of static and then a muffled sneeze told him he had got through to the dispatcher.

"Kimberly, this is the sheriff. I want a forensic team here at the cabin on Wagon Trail Road on the double. It may be crucial to our investigation."

Millie came out of the car, leaned against it with a moody expression. "I am so ready for this day to end."

After clearing her throat, Sparks opened her notebook and started scribbling in it. "I understand how you must feel, but I need to ask you some questions."

"Ms. Dozier, what time did you get here?"

"It was around twelve-thirty this afternoon, just after I got run off Sellersville Drive by a red pickup truck. No good. Very bad day," she replied.

"Walk me through what happened."

Sparks methodically wrote everything she said down, including her contact information, then cleared her to leave.

When Millie got into her car, a clap of thunder was followed by a steady succession of lightning flashes. As she drove away, she saw Sheriff Kirkman in her rearview mirror. As he stood there motionless, the lightning flashes seemed to disappear right into the earth directly behind him. He followed her with his eyes until she disappeared out of sight.

Chapter 21

ANOTHER RUMBLE of thunder reached them, and the sheriff felt a breeze pass him by. He paused to study the sky. The dark clouds were closer and heavier, becoming increasingly threatening. By the way of things, rain was inevitable. He looked away as another growl of thunder was heard.

Kirkman took a second to look at his wristwatch; they had been at this place for a little over an hour. He turned to face his deputies, Shipley, and Sparks. They were standing by the front door of the cabin and conversing in low tones among themselves. At that moment a squad car and science-support van pulled into the driveway. Two police officers immediately got out of the squad car and walked up to the cabin.

Lightning broke the sky as if it were a cracking shell. This was followed by a deafening explosion of thunder.

Then a barrage of rain pelted the ground, lifting dust as it struck. The two police officers scrambled to their vehicle to grab their rain slickers. Shipley and Sparks ducked inside the cabin, and the forensic team had yet to leave their van.

The sudden rush of rain falling on Kirkman, roused a sudden feeling of anger in him. He cast his eyes downward, knowing how this would affect the search for Abigail Wincoff. If there was anything to make the situation worse, it was a steady rain. The awful rain, the missing girl, and the earlier sight of her grieving parents — images that flashed through his thoughts as he shook his head in disappointment, then headed into the cabin.

A short while later, the forensic team were working inside the cabin. And outside the sheriff and his deputies donned rain slickers — courtesy of the two police officers who, coincidentally, happened to have extra slickers in their squad car. The two officers were now stationed on either side of the cabin.

"If we don't find her soon, we'll have to widen the search," Kirkman said to the deputies.

The sheriff reached into his shirt pocket and pulled out a topographical map of the area where Abigail Wincoff had disappeared. He used an index finger to trace Wagon Trail Road. Then he pointed to a spot on the map indicating a direction they should take.

"There's another cabin set back from Wagon Trail Road a bit. Find out if the guests know anything. Ask them if they saw anything unusual before she went missing. Then go back out and keep searching the woods," the sheriff told them, as the rain began falling harder.

Sparks looked at where his finger was pointing, then turned to look at a dirt path to her left.

"Right on it, sheriff," Deputy Sparks said with a nod.

"Shipley and Sparks, I want you two to check the woods around that cabin too."

"Will do," Shipley said, and headed toward the dirt path, eyes on the ground as the rain beat at them so hard that it was like standing in a shower.

"This weather isn't helping any," Sparks said and began walking alongside him.

"That may be the least of our worries. The sheriff would like to see this solved by the end of the week. Last year the police department's record for solving cases stood at seventy percent. If we don't do better, an angry mob of citizens are likely to elect a new sheriff before the upcoming November election, forcing Sheriff Kirkman into an even earlier retirement," Deputy Shipley said.

"It's Tuesday. That doesn't give us much time," she replied.

"Better get moving then, Deputy Sparks!" he said, as they hurried through the woods.

With the rain blowing in all directions, Kirkman walked down the dirt driveway to Wagon Trail Road. He stopped and studied the ground. The only tire tracks on the road were made by the tires of an automobile, his guess was a Toyota, Millie Dozier's car. He glanced around at the ground under his feet and back up the road. After one more glance at the ground, he spotted a partial footprint, a hint of boot tread in a patch of soft dirt. Though, he was unable to measure its size, and the water was accumulating at a rapid pace.

Back at the cabin, an older male technician puffed out sprays of black fingerprint powder from a small rubber bulb, working along a wooden window frame. Then he used the fingerprint brush to delicately brush away all of the excess powder.

In the kitchen, a young female technician walked to the sink and pumped Luminol again and again, hoping to find traces of the intruder's blood. The drain glowed with a fluorescent blue glow. She saw the path the blood had taken as it washed down the drain, then swabbed the sink with phenolphthalein. In seconds, the swab turned pink — blood. More often than not, a lot of criminals left their DNA at the scene of the crime. It was just a matter of knowing where to look. Assuming the blood was the intruder's, she packed the Q-tip away hopeful they would get something after analysis back at the lab.

When she turned around, she was certain she saw the shadow of a girl move past the entrance to the kitchen. She stepped into the doorframe to look around. She couldn't see anyone, but she could feel a presence; someone was very close.

"Hello? Is somebody there?" the technician asked in an apprehensive voice.

The moments passed in silence.

What would a little girl be doing here? she asked herself. She must have imagined it. She must have had more to drink the night before than she realized.

She found her coworker outside examining the pieces of glass on the ground. Part of her wanted to tell him what she had seen. But what had she seen? She wasn't sure of anything anymore. Instead, she told him about the blood splatter in the sink. After notifying the sheriff, she nevertheless continued her work, taking photographs of the fluorescent pattern in the kitchen sink.

Chapter 22

UNDER the drenching downpour, Deputy Shipley and Deputy Sparks had been walking in the woods around the Wincoff's cabin for almost half an hour now. Before that they'd visited a cabin set a bit back from Wagon Trail Road and spoke to a honeymooning couple. At the time Abby went missing, the honeymooners claimed they were in the cabin, but they hadn't seen or heard anything unusual.

As Shipley stepped over a downed log, his feet crunching on dead branches, he heard Deputy Sparks shout. "Over here."

The sheriff and half a dozen officers ran to surround her.

"Any sign of her?" Kirkman was quick to ask.

Sparks shook her head. "No."

Then Sparks pointed to the ground where the rain was falling heavily on a pair of binoculars lying there. Abigail Wincoff's binoculars. There was no doubt in that.

"Good work in finding them. It's a start, anyway," the sheriff said after briefly looking at the torn strap. "But is that all there is?"

Shipley, who was standing next to him, said, "It's all we've got so far. Naturally we'll keep combing the area."

"At least we know she was here. But where is she now?" he asked tersely.

"Good question," Deputy Shipley said, drily.

From the looks of things, there seemed to be foul play involved in the missing-girl case. The torn strap of the binoculars was a good indication they were forcibly removed. It wasn't a promising sight, indicating she had been abducted or murdered.

The sheriff took a step back to let Sparks pass to take some photos with her Canon EOS 5D Mark III digital SLR camera. He gazed around looking for anything out of place, or any other clue as to what happened to Abigail Wincoff. Then he sighed a deep, almost theatrical sigh reminiscent of frustration, watching Sparks. Her delicate hands moved with quick precision as she bagged the binoculars properly and cataloged it into evidence.

Meanwhile, inside the cabin, Gillian was standing by the living room window, speechless, watching the officers scurry back and forth, listening to occasional shouts punctuated by the crackling of static from radios. The seconds ticked by, the old grandfather clock in the corner marking each one. The repetitive sound only added to her anxiety. She felt paralyzed by fear and uncertainty and seemed unable to grasp the reality of her feelings. It hardly seemed possible that so much had happened in such a short amount of time that she could barely catch a thought to examine it before another one popped out. What had happened to her daughter? Was she gone for good?

Deputy Missy Sparks came out of the woods. She was walking toward a police car parked in front of the cabin. In her hand was a large Ziploc bag holding a pair of binoculars. Gillian recognized them as hers, needed to ask questions, and ran out the door of the cabin.

She hurried up to the deputy. "Those are mine. Abby used them for birdwatching."

Every muscle tensed as she stared at the evidence bag in the deputy's hand. Her stomach turned as images of Abby assaulted her brain all in the space of seconds. Abby was so sweet and innocent. She didn't like where her thoughts were taking her. She didn't like it at all.

Concern rippled across Sparks' face. "I'm afraid this is evidence now. Ma'am, please go back into the cabin. You should get out of the rain."

Ignoring the rain pouring down on her, Gillian tried to keep what little she had left inside somewhat intact and functional. "Where did you find them?"

"Lying on the ground in the woods a quarter of a mile away," she said and popped the trunk on the police cruiser to put the bag inside.

"Any sign of my daughter?" she asked in a trembling voice and swallowed hard as though struggling to contain her emotions.

Sparks looked directly into her eyes and told her the truth. "Unfortunately, not. There is no sign of her. I know it's troubling you as a parent not knowing where your child is. But with Sheriff Andy Kirkman in charge, you can be sure that the search is in good hands. So, take a breath, and go back inside. You'll be notified if we find anything else."

Gillian managed to meet her gaze and saw sincerity and concern there. "I want to know, even if it's the smallest detail."

"Sure will, ma'am," she said, slamming the trunk shut, and took off into the woods.

Since Abby's disappearance that morning, her mother had been on edge. Now it was beginning to take its toll. Soaked and shivering, her body was telling her to take a break as she closed the door of the cabin behind her. She knew she had to listen. But first she leaned against the door, her palms flat against it on either side of her body, her cheek pressed against the wood, and said a short prayer for the stress to subside. Then she took a deep breath and sighed.

When she turned around, there was her husband, standing in the middle of the living room, holding a towel in his hands. He came toward her slowly and she collapsed against him.

He helped dry her off, comforting her as best he could. "You need to change out of those wet clothes."

She nodded. "I just need a minute."

"I saw you talking to the officer from the window. Any developments?"

She looked at him, her pupils and irises blending, giving her eyes a piercing quality. "They found the binoculars."

His face drained of color as he asked, "What?"

It was like a sock to the stomach. Something like a shiver overtook him. The doubts he'd had before hearing this were all instantly pushed to the side at the thought of someone harming his daughter. But then he hadn't really understood, as he did now, what the word horror meant.

Gillian turned to him, awkwardly staring at him for a moment as if trying to decide something, then carried on talking calmly. "Don't look so panicked. That sheriff — uh, Kirkman — is scrabbling around like a rabid crab. Neither he nor his officers have gotten anywhere during the past two hours. Otherwise, they would've told us. Abby is still out there somewhere, probably just lost track of the time, and was waiting for the rain to stop."

Her statement was full of unrealistic hope, the belief that Abby had just been out playing somewhere and was coming back.

"I'm really at a loss for words. I think we should prepare for the worst, every parent's worst nightmare," Lance said, his face grave.

Their eyes met. Silence filled the room as the impact of the words sank in.

A deep sinking feeling filled her stomach. "No honey! I can't."

Lance looked at her sadly, with a tinge of fear in his sadness. "I know it's a terrible thing to say. But we must be ready for it. If the police find Abby, there's a good chance she won't be alive."

Her husband was right. But she wasn't ready to accept it. Tears came to her eyes, and she reached out and grabbed his wrist, as if she wanted to make sure he wouldn't vanish too. They were so brokenhearted — and they stayed that way for some time.

"Well, I think I'll go and change my clothes," she said as she turned toward the bedroom.

Lance stayed in the living room rather than follow her. He tossed the towel on the coffee table and sank into the couch. As he closed his eyes, he let the misery torrent through him.

Chapter 23

MUCH LATER a forensic team was erecting a blue tent over the scene where the binoculars were found. It was quite possible, Sheriff Kirkman contended, that trace evidence could have been left behind. And if there was any speck of evidence there, try as he might, the sheriff was determined to prevent the rain from washing it away. The technicians were doing their best to sift through the muddy soil and maintain a positive attitude. But parts of the ground were covered in three inches of water and the prospects were growing dim.

"If someone took her, there's nothing to show it. I'm not finding anything," a technician informed the sheriff.

Kirkman listened but didn't say anything. He looked down at the muddy ground. And for one bitter, desperate moment he cursed under his breath, convinced he was resigned to the reality that there was no evidence to recover.

At six o'clock that evening the rain let up, then returned twenty-five minutes later with renewed vigor. At that time, the sheriff finally called it a day. Before leaving, he delegated duties to his deputies planning to continue the search for Abigail Wincoff with a skeleton crew of police officers to work into the late hours of the evening.

A thin film of water covered Sellersville Drive, glistening like oil. The rain was pelting hard against the windshield of the sheriff's SUV, and he turned the wipers on full blast. And every passing vehicle sent up a blinding spray of rain and wind.

As he drove, Kirkman thought of the pain the Wincoffs must be in. A fist of ice closed around his heart. Part of his problem was that his own daughter was two years older than Abigail Wincoff, who reminded him of her for some reason. What would he do if she disappeared out of his life? The pain would be excruciating.

Please, Jesus, be with the Wincoffs in their time of grief, he prayed. *Please, Jesus, keep them safe and guide them through this difficult period.*

In the deepening twilight, shadows of a group of uniformed police officers were combing the woods surrounding the Wincoffs cabin. Gazing through the rain-spotted window in the kitchen, Gillian sighed as she watched a jagged spear of lightning split the sky. She was thinking that her daughter was out there somewhere. She hoped Abby was safe. She was dry. Well, fairly warm, not outside in the rain. Consumed by her thoughts and fears, she wiped her index finger down the condensation on the window.

She came out of her thoughts when her husband suggested she rest, which she nodded in agreement and retreated to the living room. The day's drama had exhausted her energy, leaving her devoid of speech.

Lance listened to her walk down the hallway to the living room.

Next, he heard something hit the living room floor.

Shoes.

And then the squeak of springs.

She had laid out on the couch.

Lastly came the sobs, exploding out of her body as if they'd finally found the exit that easily reached all the way to the kitchen.

Unable to endure the ringing of her grief in his own ears, he felt himself trembling and began to prepare some tea to settle their nerves. He knew the situation was the worst they had ever faced.

Gillian sat curled up on the couch, just staring into the fireplace, her mind filled with worry. She'd been so busy praying for her daughter's return, she hadn't stopped to think whether her prayers would be answered. Partly because they only went to church on Christmas and Easter. Ever since the birth of Abby, she and her husband found themselves too busy to attend Catholic mass. Now she wondered if God was punishing her. A thought or two later, and she put her face in her hands, trembling, and cried silently.

The kettle began to whistle. Lance took it off the burner, took down two mugs from the cabinet, poured boiling water over the tea bags, and added sugar and milk.

Gillian's weeping was disturbed by her husband with an offer of tea. She graciously accepted it.

"I always thought that this was God's country, peaceful country living with fresh air, lakes, mountains, and wildlife in a friendly, small-town atmosphere. Things like this aren't supposed to happen in small towns like this. Now, I wish we'd never come here," she said, rather melancholy.

"It's too late. We're already here," he said, his voice so soft it was almost lost, and then he added, "Let's have some dinner, shall we? You need to keep up your strength. And you may feel a little better afterward."

"I don't think so," Gillian said hopelessly. "I don't think anything is going to make me feel any better right now. But, if you insist, can you heat up that leftover she-crab soup for me?"

"Of course, I'll get it ready for you. Just follow me to the kitchen."

Good to his word, he heated up the soup and warmed up some bread for them both. It was a light meal but tasty and filling. And they ate in silence, not looking at each other, as if somehow it was disrespectful to be eating at a time like this.

With a sigh she got up from the kitchen table and went to the living room window to peer out. It was storming with wild winds. Spidery thin-legged, vibrant blue streaks of lightning were crawling out from under a low gray layer of clouds, not striking downward but darting horizontally across the sky. Sporadic booms of thunder seemed to form an uneasy coincidence with the beats of her aching heart. She watched the rain bucketing down, trying to make sense of it all, when there was no sense to it. Her daughter was gone. Plain and simple.

Thereafter, she retired to bed when her husband was on his cell phone talking with his mother Stella, who lived with his father, Jimmy, in a townhouse in Riverdale, New York. After telling her that Abby had gone missing, his mother didn't take the news well. She didn't speak for about a minute, instead she just listened and occasionally said "yes." She even cried — though she tried to hide it. From then on, she tried to sound optimistic.

Static interfered, his voice drifting in and out. The call didn't last very long, only four or five minutes before he clicked off because the static only got worse.

For a stretch of time he lingered, feeling deep inside him that his daughter was gone for good. He peered out of the living room window, then extinguished the fire in the fireplace before turning in for the night.

He did not sleep much of course. After a few fitful hours of rest, he rose and stared out the window wondering about Abby. Then he showered and dressed.

It was not yet seven in the morning when Gillian woke with a sudden gasp, sitting bolt upright in bed, eyes wide. She noticed the rain had stopped; early morning sunlight filtered between the curtains. And the smell of coffee told her Lance was in the kitchen.

She climbed out of bed, exhausted. It wasn't until around two that she had drifted off to sleep. She threw on a robe and headed to the bathroom. Her reflection in the mirror appeared gaunt and pale. Shocked, she sucked in a breath, staring at the dark shadows under her eyes from worry and little sleep. It didn't help either, that somewhere deep inside of her, hope of finding Abby had dimmed.

"I'm a mess," she said very softly.

When she came into the kitchen, she found that Lance had put the kettle on and laid the breakfast stuff out on the kitchen table for her. She sat down, and noticed he had a Ziploc of tea bags in his hand. Suddenly she thought about the police officer carrying a Ziploc bag holding her binoculars — the ones she had given to Abby. Close to crying, she started to pick at her food.

Chapter 24

THAT MORNING just before eight, there appeared to be a sole occupant of the chestnut log cabin on Wagon Trail Road. People were keen to visit the popular resort area in the East, even though, less than twenty-four hours earlier, the area had been rocked by reports of a missing child.

After yesterday's rain, today's air was pleasantly fresh and cool. There wasn't a cloud in the sky. And the sun was almost touching the horizon, its waning rays glistened on the moist saffron-yellow petals of the sunflowers. It was a perfect day for birdwatching.

Gail was intensely interested in the various birds that lived in the woods surrounding the cabin on Wagon Trail Road. Birdwatching. It was her hobby. A break from her writing. She was here to work on her novel — a book about a serial killing, which could put her on the path to becoming a major American writer. The title: *Murder in the Poconos.*

She wrote her first story when she was in third grade at the Bayberry Elementary School — a space adventure — and knew she wanted to be a writer. With this debut novel, she hoped one day to be called the American equivalent of Agatha Christie. She'd start with this book and maybe a few more after that. She wasn't sure just yet. It was too early for her to decide, reminding herself often that she was only in her late twenties.

She made the most of her time on a happy birdwatching outing. She was comforted by the songs of the twittering birds overhead in the trees. Her head swiveled back and forth at every sound. Loving the outdoors, at one with nature. It was as if she'd never felt so alive.

A flock of birds fluttered between trees off to her right. She raised the binoculars to her eyes and adjusted the focus knob with her finger to get a bird to come into view: white markings around the eye and a yellow rump patch. A magnolia warbler. Ten minutes later, she lowered the binoculars and draped the strap over her neck. She had enjoyed every moment of watching, but it was time to return to her writing.

Her spirits rose as she approached the cabin. Locked in the moment, she walked with a bounce in her step. All seemed right for the five foot five inches tall, slim, average-looking brunette, with a round face, and a beauty mark above her lip.

She stopped halfway to the front door and turned her head. At the corner of her eye, she thought she caught movement in one of the narrow windows at the front of the cabin. Her eyes focused on the spot where she could have sworn, she saw the curtain shift.

"Is anyone in there?" Gail asked the question out loud, not expecting an answer and not receiving one.

Gail kept her eyes locked on the spot, but the curtains remained closely drawn. Then she let her eyes wander across the other windows, including the one that had been replaced, wondering if the person inside suspected they'd been seen. Logically, she thought, they might take another vantage point.

There was no movement or sound.

One minute passed and then another while she stood silent, listening to birds chirping in the nearby woods. Glancing all about, she couldn't force her eyes to see it again, though she felt someone was watching her.

Two goldfinches flew from the white, barn-shaped birdhouse hanging from one of the branches of a pine tree beside the living-room window near the cabin's front door. The sudden wing flapping scared her even more.

Clearly her imagination was running wild. She decided the movement must have been her own. When she'd walked past the window, a flicker of her shadow fell on the glass. But just to be on the safe side, once inside, she would check the place thoroughly.

In the massive cathedral-ceilinged living room were heavy curtains that hung around the two windows and matched an enormous white suede couch covered in corduroy throw pillows, which matched the two wingback chairs in design and fabric pattern. On a polished veneer side table, there was an old, bulky manual typewriter. The oak floor was mostly covered with a black, gold, and cream Oriental rug. Most impressive was the two story-high stone fireplace. It was quaint, and comfortable for anyone seeking the peace and solitude of the countryside of Pennsylvania.

As expected, Gail hadn't found anyone inside the cabin. She slipped on a pink cardigan over her crisp tan slacks and short-sleeved white blouse dotted with pink and red flowers. Feeling giddy with anticipation, she plonked herself down in a chair in front of the typewriter and fed a sheet of paper into it. The roller was stuck. Something she hadn't anticipated. But not for too long. Relentlessly, she fiddled with the roller until she got it unjammed. To her good fortune, its keys worked. She dusted the typewriter off with the sleeve of her cardigan and began to bang out a few pages of her novel. It was clear her mind was completely in the story. Apart from her recent scare with a possible intruder, which seemed to have faded with the tranquility of the rural cabin, she seemed to feel a sense of personal purpose as a budding writer.

In the trees behind the cabin a crow cawed three times into the stillness as it flapped its wings and soared upward. It was startled in its flight by the sight of something that should not be: a figure emerging from the ground.

The figure took shape of a girl in a thin, short-sleeved, simple white dress. Ghostly in appearance, she sat hunched-over on the ground, her back against the tree. She was playing with a doll. Whispering sounds were heard. These seemed to be made by this apparition.

It was only when the ghost lifted her head up from the doll that her face was recognizable. It was Abigail Wincoff, haunting the spot where she'd been murdered.

By the time the crow landed in a tree further away, the ghost of Abby had disappeared almost as quickly as she'd appeared. A faint breeze stirred the grass where she'd been sitting.

There came a faint voice. "Help me."

Chapter 25

NOT FAR FROM the Monroe County Courthouse, a black-and-white flyer of the missing Abigail Wincoff was affixed to a utility pole on Monroe Street in Stroudsburg, Pennsylvania. A snappy wind blew along the street and made the top of the flyer flap. Nearly twenty feet in the air, there were dozens of black birds preening and chirping on the power lines attached to the wooden pole. Most were crows. Some starlings and redwing blackbirds.

Shortly after nine, Sheriff Kirkman was in his office and at his computer when Chief Deputy Aubrey Livengood came in for their usual morning briefing.

"What's happening?" Livengood asked, placing a sheaf of papers on the sheriff's desk before taking a seat in one of the two guest chairs facing his desk.

Kirkman got up, walked over to the door, and pulled it shut. He sat back down in his chair and looked at Livengood across his desk.

For the next twenty minutes or so, they discussed routine departmental business, including yesterday's incident reports. The meeting ended with a discussion of the Abigail Wincoff disappearance now into its second day.

"The lab confirmed that the blood found in the kitchen sink of the cabin on Wagon Trail Road proved to be the same blood type as that of Abigail Wincoff. So, I've sent over a forensic guy to get DNA samples of her from her parents to make an exact match, but it's her blood alright," Livengood said.

"Besides the blood, did forensics pick up anything else?" Kirkman pressed.

"Prints and DNA were recovered from the binoculars. And a partial footprint highlighted by the UV scan on Wagon Trail Road. Hiking boots. Could be either a tall man or a large woman."

"Or possibly a juvenile," the sheriff suggested.

"This morning Deputy Missy Sparks will be organizing a careful, inch-by-inch search of the property surrounding the Wincoff's cabin. There's a good chance that the person who may have abducted Abigail stalked around the cabin beforehand. Any physical evidence left behind by the perp, would likely be outside the Wincoff's cabin rather than inside it," Livengood said.

Sheriff Kirkman nodded. "The whole thing infuriates me. The Wincoffs came here on vacation and in a matter of minutes this happy, comfortable family suddenly had their lives turned upside down."

Chief Deputy Livengood seemed a little taken aback by the strength of his emotion. "So, then what's the next step?"

"Tell the deputies that I want to meet with them later this afternoon. I want an update on where we stand on the Abigail Wincoff case."

"I'll get right to it," Livengood said.

With the briefing over, the chief deputy opened the door and sauntered out of his office. Through the open doorway, Kirkman sat looking down the hallway that led to the interior lobby and the glass cubicle of the department's secretary and dispatcher.

A short moment later, Kimberly Kaasa entered to set down the day's mail on his desk. The attractive black woman in her early thirties turned toward him with barely a smile and without so much as a word before she left and returned to her cubicle.

In an effort to keep himself busy, he reviewed some of the papers on his desk regarding recent incidents in his jurisdiction. The trouble was he couldn't erase from his mind the Abigail Wincoff case. The fact that little progress had been made. Thoughts about the scene outside the Wincoff's cabin yesterday were racing through his head as he tackled the paperwork, wanting to leave it in some kind of reasonable order.

It was nearly three fifteen that afternoon when he finished sorting through a pile of papers. That was about the time when his phone rang.

"Deputies Shipley and Sparks are here," the dispatcher announced.

"Thanks Kimberly. Send them in," he leaned an elbow on the desk and rested his forehead in his open palm.

The sheriff's gut said this meeting could get out of sorts. It also said he needed to keep his temper under control. Sure enough, the deputies walked in and got right into it. For a while he listened to them talk in front of him.

"Six hours," cut in Deputy Sparks. "That's how long we've been searching. No physical evidence. Zero."

"That's not long enough," Kirkman said in his blunt way. "Get back out there and keep looking!"

That last line came out louder than he'd intended, his tone louder. The door to his office was open. He could see a few heads in the lobby turn his way for a half second. Even Kimberly crept to the end of her cubicle to peek out.

His face burned as the deputies started talking over one another. He closed his eyes briefly, simply trying to hold his temper. Then he held up a hand, cutting them off.

"One at a time," he said before banging a paperweight against the side of his desk.

"I don't think we're going to find any physical evidence of the perp — blood or hair or prints. I'm guessing the rain washed it away," Shipley said flatly.

"I'd like to know whether Abigail Wincoff has been kidnapped or abducted — or if she's been murdered. And if she has been murdered, I want her body to be found by Friday night, so I don't have to spend Saturday worrying about it. Is there any chance of that happening? Or maybe that's just wishful thinking on my part," the sheriff said in impatient tones.

Shipley hitched up his duty belt. "I am all for that, sheriff — but try as we might, I don't think it's going to happen in that short amount of time."

Kirkman folded his arms, staring. He truly hoped that Deputy Shipley was wrong.

"Keep looking!" the sheriff said, holding back his rising temper.

It wasn't a question or even a suggestion. The deputies left the room with looks of frustration on their faces.

An hour or so later, when the sheriff's day was almost over, the phone rang. Assuming that Kimberly would answer it, he let it ring several times until he realized it was ten minutes after six. His secretary, Kimberly Kaasa — a working mother of two toddlers in day care and a husband who also worked — clocked out at five-thirty each afternoon. Sighing, he picked up the phone.

"Hi, Andy," Merrilee Kirkman said. "How's your day been?"

He shivered with pleasure upon hearing his wife's voice on the phone.

"My head is starting to ache," he said and touched his temple. "Other than that, I'm peachy keen."

"Should I hold your dinner? It's meat loaf," she asked.

"Yeah, keep it warm for me. It gives me something to look forward to when I get home."

"Okay. Well, then, see you when you get home. Love you," she said endearingly to him.

"I love you the same," he said and hung up the phone.

It was now approaching 6:30 P.M. With no other calls or emergencies, he was ready to turn in for the day.

Chapter 26

IN THOSE FIRST DAYS the police grew increasingly frustrated. They were getting nervous. Missing children weren't a common occurrence in the Poconos. Places where the big-money people spent their summer vacations. There were no leads as to where Abigail Wincoff was. Where was her body if someone had killed her? They found her blood. But that didn't mean she was dead.

Now it was Friday morning, three days since Abby's disappearance.

Gillian Wincoff was unshowered, in an open bathrobe covering a flannel nightgown and looked like a woman from an asylum. She was standing in the doorway of the bedroom watching her husband stuff some clothes and his toiletry bag into a suitcase. Their five-night stay was over. They were going to vacate the cabin and return to their home in New Jersey. In a little over a week, Gillian planned to return and stay a week or two in a hotel in Stroudsburg. The trip would be for the sake of following the case of her missing daughter, checking in with the sheriff and waiting around for any developments.

Lance zipped up the suitcase and pulled it down off the bed. When he turned back to the doorway, his wife was gone. He heard her walking down the hallway, dialing a number on her cell phone. He stooped, hefted the suitcase, and made his way out of the room.

The phone rang in Sheriff Kirkman's office. After answering, he was frustrated to find out it was Abigail Wincoff's mother. At this point in the investigation, he wasn't ready to talk to her. He listened to her greeting patiently, masking his annoyance with a polite expression.

"In my absence, I'm counting on the police to find her and return her to my home in Watchung, New Jersey," she said in a rising voice.

"We'll do our best, and we'll keep looking for her, Mrs. Wincoff," he said blandly.

"Tell me the truth," said Gillian hoarsely, and asked in a desperate way, "what do your instincts tell you? Is my daughter dead?"

The sheriff had an obligation to be truthful. But in this challenging time when people were most vulnerable and desperately hanging onto hope — that was something he didn't want to take away from her.

"It is still too early in the case to start theorizing. Let's not get ahead of ourselves. I'm heading over to the cabin. I want to see you off," the sheriff stated insistently.

"Fine. I'll see you later then," she murmured before disconnecting the call.

The sheriff slapped the pen he'd been writing notes with down on the desk and sat back. It was all he could do to keep from fidgeting in nervous frustration. He inhaled deeply and shrugged his shoulders, shaking himself out of his funk. *What now?* he thought.

"Anybody else have something to add about the case?" the sheriff asked himself ironically.

Andy Kirkman, who was with the Highway Patrol, an elite unit of the Philadelphia Police Department, years before he relocated to Stroudsburg and got elected sheriff, liked his line of work. On the rare weekends he wasn't working, he was with his wife, Merrilee, and teenage daughter or doing house chores. He recently went through a rough patch in his marriage, but they worked it out. And he looked forward to retirement — devoting himself to his wife, whom he dearly loved after twenty-four years together.

As far back as high school, when he'd met his sweetheart turned wife, he'd always maintained a muscular physique with little effort. Now in his early forties, his muscles were beginning to sag. He considered himself lucky if he managed to break away once or twice a week to lift weights since becoming sheriff of Monroe County. And his cardio workout was limited to the unremitting pace of his job. But now, with his retirement around the corner, he would have plenty of time to get himself in better shape.

As he gathered himself to leave, his thoughts were still preoccupied with the Abigail Wincoff case, even as he walked out of his office. What upset him the most was that there was no definitive clue about what happened to Abby.

Of course, he suspected foul play but there were no suspects, no prints, and no DNA. Nobody seemed to have seen or heard anything. But that didn't surprise him. The Wincoff's cabin was secluded in the woods, like most of the other cabins in the Poconos. That was why the tourists liked it. The seclusion gave them a chance to unplug from the grind of their daily lives. And unfortunately, that worked to the advantage of any criminal mind.

Sheriff Kirkman climbed into his SUV and just sat with his hands on the steering wheel and stared out the windshield. His eyebrows pinched into a frown, thinking back to his phone call with Gillian Wincoff. All along, his instincts told him that Abby was most likely dead. He had a nagging feeling about the case he couldn't shake. *There were only two real possibilities with the Wincoff disappearance*, he thought. She was killed by a stranger, or a traveling killer passing through that went from city to city and picked her out because of her type. Or she was killed for a reason. The fact that the body was missing was proof that she was killed by a traveler. And the killer might be days away before the body was found.

He couldn't share this with Gillian Wincoff, not when it was just speculation.

And he felt for Abigail Wincoff. Over the years, he'd seen too many dead children. Toddlers beaten to death by their parents; unwanted babies in garbage cans; teenagers who shot themselves accidentally when playing with their father's gun they'd found in a closet. No matter how often it happened, he never got used to it.

He started the ignition of the Expedition and throttled the air conditioner. His eyebrows were still squished together, when he drove out of the parking space, which seemed to suit his melancholy mood.

Chapter 27

OUTSIDE THE WINCOFF'S CABIN, a news van, BRC TV13 out of Lehighton, was setting up near to where a female uniformed deputy was standing at attention. The deputy squinted in the direction of the angle of the camera, which was positioned in a way that showed her in the background.

TV Anchorwoman and reporter Kristi Maratos was already out of the van. She glimpsed herself in her silver compact mirror and began working on her pink lipstick with a small black brush.

Inside the van, the engineer guy glanced at the line-monitor that showed the live feed fed back to the station while his hands worked the switcher controls.

"Stand by Kristi. We're live in thirty seconds," the cameraman said.

After rubbing her lips together, she snapped the compact shut, dropped it in her black DKNY handbag. She walked over to the van and set her handbag on the passenger seat. Then she took her position in front of the camera with the handheld microphone.

As though her quirky charm was made for television, Kristi Maratos was a stunning girl with a figure that made men stop dead in their tracks. Her exquisite legs and body always demanded a second look. It didn't hurt that she never went anywhere without looking her best — hair, makeup, and clothing, the whole shebang.

Kristi fluffed her hair and looked directly into the camera. "I'm Kristi Maratos here in East Stroudsburg outside the cabin where Abigail Wincoff had been staying with her parents until her disappearance three days ago. Abigail Wincoff is twelve years old, with sandy brown hair and eyes, and was last seen somewhere in the vicinity of this cabin off Sellersville Drive. She was here on vacation with her parents. The police have searched the cabin and grounds, but they found no clues to the girl's whereabouts. Anyone with information on her whereabouts, is urged to contact the Pennsylvania State Police."

Just then Sheriff Kirkman pulled his Expedition into the driveway of the cabin. The driver's door swung wide open, and he emerged in uniform, and with a file in his hand. He drew a quick breath as he turned his weary eyes to the cabin before walking up to the front door.

"Hello," she was saying as she hurried up to the sheriff with the TV cameraman in tow. "I'm Kristi Maratos, BRC

TV13 News. We're here seeking information about the disappearance of Abigail Wincoff —"

The sheriff waved his hand. "No comment, I'm sorry."

In a flash, the sheriff stopped in his tracks and opened his file folder. He took out a thin stack of flyers about the missing Abigail Wincoff and handed them to her.

"Take these and pass them around," the sheriff said before continuing on his way.

Kirkman knocked on the door of the cabin and was let in by Lance Wincoff.

Not even a second later, Deputy Shipley stepped out of the woods to confront the news crew. The look on his face was that of impatience and concern.

"How much longer are you going to be here?" the deputy asked the two of them waiting to see who would answer.

Kristi walked up to him and said, "We just wrapped."

When he looked at her, those greenish eyes of his seemed to look right into her soul. And she liked it. This caught her off guard. She wondered if it was intentional or just his way of looking at her in the heat of the moment. No more than that.

The cameraman shied off at that point, merely murmuring: "I'll put the camera away."

"That's good to know. Well, I'm off, then," Shipley said rather hesitantly as he caught a glimmer in her eye and took in her appearance, which he found quite attractive, then offered, rather gallantly. "My name is Deputy Billy

Shipley. If there's any assistance which I can render, please don't hesitate to find me."

She felt his words had a softness. Nervous about what to say next, her eyes fell to the ground.

"I will certainly do that. Nice to meet you, by the way," was all that she said, briefly looking up as he stepped away.

Men really liked her, which was something of an understatement. She knew she was hot. Men became weak-kneed and stupid around her. But in Deputy Shipley's case, he didn't fixate on her as he was preoccupied with his job. This intrigued her.

"Likewise," he said with his back turned and a casual wave of his hand.

A little rough, she thought, *but incredibly attractive*. He must be dating someone.

Judging from the tension in her chest, her heart was fluttering. This encounter had her thoughts and feelings all twisted. She realized right then and there that she wanted someone in her life. *A tough realization that she didn't want to be alone*, she thought.

Kristi casually glanced in Shipley's direction as he walked toward the cabin. She tried not to stare outright, shamelessly checking him out like this. *He had a nice walk*, she thought. Confident and assertive.

Deputy Shipley's image popped into her mind. His face, shoulders, and hands. Shipley, God, what was wrong with her? She was acting like a teenager with a crush, but she couldn't help herself. It wasn't like she couldn't do with a little friendship.

The click of the closing door of the van shook her from her thoughts. The cameraman had settled into a comfortable position behind the wheel, while the engineer guy had taken his seat in the back of the van. She shrugged her shoulders in a "never mind" sort of way, moved to the passenger's side of the van and climbed in.

Moments later, Kristi suggested they wait awhile as she might catch an interview with the missing girl's parents should they happen to step outside.

Chapter 28

IN THE LIVING ROOM of the cabin, the sheriff picked up a report from the file folder and looked over the paper. Lance Wincoff had left the room to check on the progress of his wife, who had just had a shower and changed into fresh clothes. Gillian was packing the last of her things in the master bedroom. Deputy Shipley was by the window closest to the door, intently watching the news crew, seemingly interested in Kristi Maratos.

"Those TV people out there had been filming the cabin and the surrounding woods," Shipley said with his back turned.

Sheriff Kirkman looked up from the report he'd been reading. "Yeah."

Deputy Shipley puckered his pale face into a knot of thought. "Should the news crew film the cabin?"

"Why not?" Kirkman answered, his eyes roving around the room, thumbnail pressed against his lip.

The sheriff's eyes stopped on the elk head hanging on the wall above the fireplace. It was hard to miss from anywhere in the room.

Shipley scratched his head and turned to face him. "I don't know. It doesn't seem right."

"Think it over. The outside of a cabin doesn't mean anything to anybody."

"If you think of it that way, yeah," Shipley said, then changed the subject abruptly. "Sorry to say, there's nothing out there on Abigail Wincoff."

A silence came over the sheriff, making Shipley uneasy; he tried not to overthink it.

"I'm quite sad to admit that I think finding her doesn't seem possible," Kirkman mumbled in a quiet, saddened voice.

Deputy Shipley gave an inward wince at his candidness, then he thought about what the sheriff said some more.

"I suppose I should have expected you to say that."

In fact, the disappearance of Abigail Wincoff seemed suspicious enough that Kirkman added gravely, "We're looking for a body now. There's no doubt about that in my mind."

"Something will give us the break we need," Deputy Shipley said in a confident tone.

"How can you be so sure?" the sheriff asked him.

"You've told me many times, even in the most difficult times, that in our line of work, failure is not an option."

"Thanks for reminding me," Kirkman smirked, then added, "Tell Chief Deputy Livengood we need to drag Meadow Lake. The killer could've dumped the body there. Let's see what the divers find."

"Okay, I'll head out now," Shipley said as he walked toward the door.

As the front door closed behind the deputy, the sheriff heard voices in the hallway — Lance Wincoff's voice wavering slightly and that of his wife.

"Okay, dear. I'll carry them for you if you'll let me," Lance suggested in a gentle manner.

The next moment, Lance walked into the living room, with Gillian following. He had her suitcase in one hand and a large red shopping bag in the other.

Lance stopped halfway to the door. "Thanks for your help, sheriff. We'll be in touch."

The sheriff only nodded in response as they both turned their gazes on Gillian, who was wearing a knee-length, light blue linen dress under a thin beige cardigan, her handbag over her shoulder. She looked so drawn, tired — her face was pale, and her eyes were bleary and unfocused.

Gillian simply stared at Sheriff Kirkman. Her cracked lips fell open, and she was about to say something to him, but caught herself and walked quickly to the door. She had nothing to say.

When Lance and Sheriff Kirkman got to the front door, Gillian put out her hand, Lance took her hand in his and they set off. Kirkman stopped in the doorway and watched them walk to their Buick. He knew that going home would be the best thing for Gillian Wincoff. How in God's name could staying in the place where her daughter disappeared, possibly do her any good?

And there she was, coming out of the passenger side of the news van. The sheriff gave Kristi Maratos the once-over, looking at her from head to toe and shaking his head in disapproval just as she glanced his way. Her eyes widened as if she was startled, then she reluctantly closed the door and settled back into the passenger's seat in the van. Sheriff Kirkman rubbed his chin, then started walking toward his SUV.

Once in the driver's seat, Lance ignored the BRC TV13 news van parked in the driveway and glanced in his wife's direction. Gillian sat slumped in the passenger's seat, staring ahead at nothing. Just as the sheriff climbed into the driver's seat of his SUV, Lance pulled away and Gillian shifted her eyes to the rearview mirror, staring at the cabin. Then she shut her eyes. Tears oozed out of their corners and ran down her cheeks.

At eleven o'clock in the morning, as the Wincoff's SUV drove down Sellersville Drive with Sheriff Kirkman's Ford Expedition following behind, Millie Dozier passed them in her white Toyota. She caught a glimpse of the sheriff's expression, staring at her with surprise. Her agency had scheduled her to clean the cabin. It was one of those rare coincidences that life sometimes sets up.

Now that the sheriff and the Wincoffs had left, Kristi Maratos and her crew were talking about whether to leave or not when Millie's car pulled into the driveway. After Millie got out of her car, Kristi took off to investigate.

"Hello," she said as she hurried over to Millie. "I'm Kristi Maratos, BRC TV13 News. I'm working on a story about the missing girl, Abigail Wincoff. What brings you to the area where the girl disappeared?"

"I'm just here to clean up and change the linens," Millie said, walking swiftly toward the cabin.

Kristi handed her a missing-child flyer with Abigail Wincoff's picture on it. "If you see her, please contact the Pennsylvania State Police."

Millie stopped walking to look it over. An inward chill spread inside her, something about Abby — not to mention her eyes and her smile — felt familiar. Where had she seen her before? She couldn't have seen her before. No — she would have remembered her. She was staring so deeply into the photograph that it looked like she was in a trance.

Kristi noticed an odd expression on her face, so she asked, "Is everything okay, miss?"

Startled out of her thoughts, Millie glanced at her, with her crossed eyes wary. "They won't find her; I know they won't."

Kristi looked rather alarmed at her response. "What makes you say that?"

She started to voice her opinion. "Somebody took her away. That somebody meant to do it. Her parents aren't going to see her again. She's no longer of this earth."

Kristi had already lost interest in the conversation and gave a reply that ended the matter abruptly. "I hope you're wrong, for the parents' sake. Thank you for sharing your thoughts with me, but I must be going."

However, Millie was still fixated on the subject. "Poor little girl. At least she is with God now."

The woman — Kristi didn't even bother to ask her name at this point — had very small, crossed eyes in her round face, she couldn't ignore. It gave the woman the strangest expression she'd ever seen. And she'd heard enough. With no more to say, she simply shrugged her shoulders and returned to the van, thinking what an odd woman that was.

Chapter 29

THE NEWS VAN pulled out of the driveway of the cabin, whipped the wheel, and drove sedately out onto Sellersville Drive. Kristi Maratos relaxed in the passenger seat and simply let her mind drift where it would. The cameraman behind the wheel turned on the stereo to drown out the earlier events around the cabin. The engineer, a chubby guy in his late twenties, was seated in the back checking the equipment. His strand of frizzy, red hair sticking out from under a blue bandanna worn piratelike around his forehead was what stood out about his appearance.

The day's events were as unpredictable as weather patterns. Kristi's mind clouded with a mix of infatuation with Deputy Billy Shipley. Her conversation with him had been too brief. She wanted another chance to talk to him.

She thought back to her last relationship a little over a year ago. Wait a second. Jesus, it was nearly two years.

They'd met online. At the time she was researching a story about the former coal-mining town of Hazleton — located 97 miles northwest of Philadelphia — that became the first city to pass an Anti-immigrant ordinance in July 2006. The ordinance had placed restrictions on the hiring of undocumented workers. Just for the heck of it, she sought out his help. It just so happened that the thirty-three-year-old, ruggedly handsome professor at Carnegie-Mellon University had a bit of knowledge on the subject. Hitting it off immediately after one email exchange, they began talking on the phone. Soon they'd formed a friendship that became something more. He'd had a girlfriend, although, as he said charmingly, he was planning to break up with her soon. Emily. Wait a second. Cassandra. It was a relationship doomed to fail from the start. He had been especially attentive to her in bed, but was too fond of ESPN, and he never broke up with Cassandra.

One day she called him at home, and a woman answered with a Spanish accent. For some reason she was reliving the conversation and chastised herself as a fool.

"Who is this?" she asked nervously.

"Cassandra, his fiancé. I live here. Who are you?" she asked in a demanding voice.

After hearing that, Kristi hung up the phone and that was the end of that.

She sighed and shifted in her seat. She really wanted to talk to Deputy Billy Shipley again. That would take some planning. She smiled to herself. She hadn't felt like this in a long time, and she nearly giggled.

Six minutes later, the van turned from Stroudsmoor Road into the parking lot of the railroad dining car restaurant, Victoria Station. It was just before noon, and everyone was looking forward to a hearty lunch.

The restaurant was filled mostly with tourists and guests of The Stroud Inn. The maître d' standing behind the podium greeted Kristi and her crew grandly and took them to one of the available tables. The train conductor looking floor manager tipped his gold-trimmed wide-brimmed hat to them, a cool smile, before returning to his roped-off area by the entrance.

It was certainly no surprise to find Estelle Rowland on duty. She swapped greetings with the maître d' who hustled past her, her arms piled with trays. The experienced waitress managed a couple of pleasantries as she distributed four separate meals around a table of tourists, dealing out plates like playing cards from a deck. It wasn't the first time she'd astonished out-of-towners by getting the right entrée, beverage, and appetizer to the right person.

A fraction of a second later, she was in the kitchen. She hurriedly put three glasses of water on a tray before heading to the news crew's table in the corner of the restaurant. Arriving there, she placed the glasses of water in front of them with an accommodating smile. Until seeing Kristi Maratos up close reminded her of the news stories about the upcoming presidential election, and her smile faded at once. It was only a few short days ago since Estelle had seen the reports splashed across the media. The upcoming election wasn't something she liked thinking about, but even as it irked her, she was accustomed to emotional restraint at work.

With effort, Estelle attempted nonchalance. "Welcome. You folks take your time looking over the menu. I'll be back in a tick."

"Before you take off, I want to give you something. Here's a flyer. Perhaps you could post it here," Kristi said, pulled a Missing Child flyer of Abigail Wincoff from her handbag and handed it to her.

Estelle took it with her right hand and slid the tray under her right arm, squeezing it against her rib cage. Her face paled when she looked at the flyer. Frozen in place, she stared deeply at the photo on the paper.

Her eyebrows shot up in surprise. "I've seen her. I'm sure of it. She was here with her parents."

"What an odd coincidence," the engineer guy said.

"It sure is," Kristi agreed with him.

But there was something more. Estelle couldn't take her eyes off the photograph. She was thinking back to that day when that creep with an attitude was staring at the girl so intensely. In the glint of his blue eyes. A weird expression on his face. Maybe as if he liked her. And now the girl was missing. He was gone, too. Could it be a coincidence? She was sure he had checked out of the inn because she hadn't seen him or his red Chevrolet Silverado in a couple of days.

And for a moment, Kristi felt outside herself, watching Estelle's eyes lose focus as she stared at the flyer. Like a déjà vu moment. It was exactly like the way that odd woman outside the cabin had reacted to it.

"Is there something else you'd like to share?" Kristi couldn't help herself. "A reporter has to ask."

Startled by the sudden question, Estelle moved the flyer away from her face. She glanced at her swiftly. Behind her glasses her eyes were twitching and starting to look like a reflection in a funhouse mirror. She didn't feel comfortable telling the TV anchorwoman her suspicions.

"Not at all. If I have anything else to say, next time Sheriff Kirkman comes in, I'll say it to him," Estelle said curtly.

For a brief instant, Kristi and her crew looked at each other, bewildered. Still Kristi sensed there was something more but said nothing in response. She knew better than to press the issue further, so she just nodded. There was always the chance she was reading more into it than was there.

"I'll go pin this flyer to the corkboard on the wall by the entrance and come back to take your orders," Estelle said professionally.

Estelle tacked up the flyer and stepped back for another look. There was no question in her mind that Abigail Wincoff was the girl that creepy man with an attitude had been ogling. And the worst part was, he looked like a pedophile right out of a TV show. He just gave off those vibes. A haunting sketch of his face still lingered in her mind, his eyes hypnotizing her. But she never found out his name. Even she couldn't imagine what her reaction would be should she see him again, except maybe to call the police on the spot.

But Estelle couldn't worry about that now. She turned around and headed toward Kristi Maratos' table. When she got there, she pulled the pen out of the knot of hair that was piled up on her head and tapped her pen against her pad.

"What can I get you all today?" Estelle quickly asked.

Chapter 30

A WHITE-THROATED SPARROW was high up on a branch of a nearby tree. Gail lifted her binoculars and watched it for a long time. Birdwatching was an emotional refuge for her and a much-needed break from her hours on the manuscript. The day was sunny and bright, exactly right for the occasion. Still, she wasn't going to spend too much time out in the woods. She wasn't here to sightsee. She came here to write a book. Her writing consumed every free moment she had but gave her a feeling of satisfaction.

She studied the bird for almost a minute longer before lifting her eyes from the binoculars and looking up at the sky. But then the most peculiar thing happened: a giggling little girl moved quickly through the woods. The girl had disappeared around the tree so fast that all she really saw was her shadow. Or at least she thought that was what she saw.

Where did she come from?

And so, quiet as the forest itself, she looked around. For an instant a light wind moved the trees, and afternoon sunlight spilled through the branches. She saw nothing more. What exactly did she see? A girl, near ten years old? She had to wonder why a little girl would be running around in the woods by herself.

Where did she go?

Gail disregarded the thought just as quickly. Deciding not to waste any more time on the matter, she started to make her way back to the cabin.

When she reached the cabin, she cast a glance at an eastern bluebird after it soared past her head. The little bird, carrying a small branch in its beak, flew to the birdhouse hanging from one of the branches of a pine tree outside the living-room window of the cabin. Much to her amusement, the eastern bluebird landed right at the entrance to the birdhouse, cautiously peered in, and finally went all the way in. It was making a nest inside the tiny house.

Her eye caught a flash of movement. She focused her attention on the woods and saw something skitter through the trees. Then she heard a girl giggling. Her brown eyes went as stormy as the winter sea, and her face froze in fear. Slowly, she scanned the area she thought she might have seen a little girl again. Twice in one day, it just couldn't be her imagination. It had to be real, or so she thought.

But she lost interest and started walking toward the front door of the cabin.

There she was.

A few steps later, Gail stopped. The little girl came into her line of sight then, standing at the edge of the cabin. She tilted her head slightly for a better look at the face of the girl wearing a thin, short-sleeved, white dress, her hand clinging to the arm of a doll. Curiosity crossed her face as she stared at Gail for several seconds. *It was possible the little girl had wandered over from a nearby cabin*, Gail thought.

The girl wore an expression of intensity. She had pallid skin and sunken dark eyes, which did not so much as blink. However, strange as she appeared, it didn't occur to Gail that the girl was a ghost. Abigail Wincoff. There was no question of it!

"Oh, hello," Gail said with a wave of her hand.

Abby waved her hand back at her but remained silent. She lowered her hand to her side, and Abby lowered her hand to her side, mimicking the gesture and puckered her face up.

Gail took one step forward, and she did the same. Abby continued mimicking her every move. It made Gail feel like she was looking in a mirror. Even more strangely, there was a profound odor in the air, like something decaying. A putrid smell of decomposing flesh was coming from Abby.

A part of Gail wanted to say something more, but for reasons she couldn't understand, she held her tongue. Her mind told her mouth to cease. All she could do was stare into Abby's empty eyes. And the longer she did, the more she felt like she herself wasn't there at all.

It could be nothing else but something supernatural afoot. Though Gail couldn't comprehend it just then.

The next thing that happened was Gail caught a glint in her eye just before she lifted the doll to her chest, hugging and rocking it in a gesture of comfort.

But then had come the startling distraction — a crow gave a loud caw. Gail looked up to see the big black bird perched on a high branch of a pine tree, looking down at her. The sun passed across her eyes, making her squint. Then, in a heartbeat, the crow was gone. Her face took on an expression of confusion. She was wondering if it had ever been there in the first place. Even more confusing was when she looked back to where Abby had stood, she was no longer there.

Gail walked around the cabin but couldn't find her anywhere. She paused to watch the woods, expecting her to reappear, but she didn't. After a long moment of looking back and forth, she gave up for good.

"I'm not wasting any more time on this foolishness," she mumbled through clenched lips.

Upon entering the cabin, she walked over to the living room window and stared out at the woods, but the girl was nowhere that she could see. Had she been imagining things?

After further consideration, she chalked it up to being alone in the cabin for days at a time. It was something she wasn't accustomed to. There was a good chance she was suffering from cabin fever. But if she continued to question herself whether she was seeing things, she thought she'd surely go mad.

Forcibly, she pushed her thoughts away by thinking about her novel — and she felt it was going very well. She was rather excited at the prospect of getting into it. For the last two mornings, she had come up with insight into the killer's character. That was becoming clearer and clearer. The killer, readers will learn early in the novel, relishes the thought of his anonymity, and savors his sense of power over his victims.

She sat down in front of the typewriter, inserted a piece of paper, and began to type furiously. And soon she started sinking deeper into the imagined world of her novel, the only place she wanted to be right now.

It was late afternoon, and the last light of the day was fading. It wasn't long after that the cabin had vanished completely into the black, moonless night. The fluttering of wings and chirping ceased. The silence evoked a feeling of mystery that spread over the cabin and everything around it. On this still evening, when there was no wind to rustle the trees around the cabin, you could clearly hear the ghostly moaning sounds coming from the apparition that was materializing.

Abby's ghost had appeared, hovering outside the cabin's living room window. All the curtains in the cabin were closed and the lights off. Her spirit was sort of murmuring, whispering to herself sounding a lot like raspy breathing.

A single black crow soared by the window interrupting her trance and then flew away into the woods, vanishing with a melancholy wail. A beat or two later, she drifted in the same direction to the woods. When she stopped, her body swayed from side to side in jerky movements. Her image blurred and then re-formed as she moved — going in and out of focus, like she was being projected.

"Help me please, Daddy, help me," Abby's spirit cried softly into the night.

Abby's ghost had suddenly vanished into thin air. Now there was nothing in that spot in the woods, the spot where she had been murdered.

Chapter 31

YESTERDAY Gillian Wincoff had returned to her home in Somerset County, New Jersey. In the ten days she had spent in a Stroudsburg hotel, she hoped, by some miracle, her daughter would turn up. It was emotionally exhausting for her. And the police in Pennsylvania could only offer their weak reassurances that they were doing all they could to find Abby.

Watchung was a sleepy little New Jersey town located within the Raritan Valley region approximately twenty-nine miles west of the boisterous New York City. It looked quaintly historic — a bunch of big, clapboard houses and yards shaded by trees, most of them oaks.

The Wincoffs lived in a modest white clapboard house on Timberline Way. The three-bedroom home was older, two stories with an attic under the roof, a cellar under the ground, and an overgrown garden with huge old oak trees in it. The garage tucked under the house and the enclosed front porch was accessible by a cracked concrete sidewalk.

With her husband at work, here she was — home alone. Still in her bathrobe, she was lying on the sofa in the living room, absorbed in depressing thoughts, a picture of Abby on a bicycle fisted in her hand. Abby's disappearance a month ago was still fresh for her.

She thought back to that day when she'd found Abby in the cabin's bedroom sitting on the edge of the bed, moping. Oh, God, how she wanted to be outside. Birdwatching. She was upset. Just like a girl her age would be expected to act.

If it had been up to Abby, she would have been outside all day long. But she was compliant to her parents' wishes by not staying outside too long. She had agreed to do so.

So why did Abby leave the cabin without telling her?

That was the burning question. Blame it on adolescence and being away from home, on vacation — she'd never have behaved like that in New Jersey. Still, she tried to tell herself that it wasn't unusual for a child to break the rules, just as she tried to tell herself that it was a part of growing up and learning.

Was her daughter going to be just another statistic like so many other missing children in America?

Gillian was still stressing about it, as one would expect a mother to do. She sighed and swept her hand through her hair. A tangle of hair fell across her eye, but she ignored it.

Somewhere inside her she knew something bad must have happened to Abby, but she wanted to keep hoping.

Lying around wallowing in pity wasn't going to help. If there was ever a time when she needed to be strong, and not weak, it was now.

Abby was going to come back, she told herself briskly. If she told herself that often enough, she might believe it. *Abby would be found soon, safe and sound*, she reassured herself as she got up from the sofa, put the picture on a side table, and headed to the kitchen.

She started to brew herself a cup of orange-pekoe tea, thinking that she had let her imagination run away with her common sense. Was she just living in fantasy thinking Abby would come back? Maybe, she acknowledged self-derisively. But then fantasy was all she had to cling to at this moment.

Sometime after lunch, she was in the bedroom, picking up her iPhone off the bedside table and scrolling through her contacts. Her face riven with tension; she dialed the number to the sheriff's office in Stroudsburg, Pennsylvania.

The sheriff's secretary answered, and she asked, "Can you put me through to Sheriff Andy Kirkman?"

"Your name?"

"Tell him it's Gillian Wincoff from Watchung, New Jersey."

Kirkman was in the hallway when he heard the phone ringing in his office. He hurried to his desk to pick it up. And when he did, he could feel a drop of sweat trickling down between his ear and the phone receiver. Before saying anything, he held the receiver away from his head and wiped his ear with his sleeve.

"Sheriff Kirkman."

"Oh, good," Kimberly Kaasa said with relief in her voice. "You're still there. I was afraid you had gone out on a call."

"I'm still here. What's up?"

"Gillian Wincoff is on the line."

"Put her through," Kirkman said, and blew out a breath in frustration. "This is Sheriff Kirkman. What can I help you with, Mrs. Wincoff?"

"I know I saw you two days ago, in Stroudsburg, but I'm desperate to know if there are any recent developments concerning my missing daughter's case."

"Not really. All I can say is that the investigation is not moving fast enough. Point is, we just don't know yet what happened to your daughter," the sheriff said, in his best professional voice.

"So, what you're telling me is that she just disappeared into thin air. I mean, I know the police have conducted countless searches for Abby. Don't you have any leads to her whereabouts?"

The tone of disappointment was unmistakable. It seemed she was implying that he didn't know how to do his job. And it made him roar inside. But he stayed calm, staring at the brass clock on his desk.

"No, we do not have any leads at this time. I know it's tough to hear. But it is what it is. Hang in there. Our investigation is moving forward. I'll keep you notified, Mrs. Wincoff. As soon as I know something, so will you."

Gillian Wincoff thanked him before disconnecting.

In his preoccupied state, he felt he needed another coffee. Not too bad, though. Only the second cup of the day. He usually had four cups in the course of any given day. It was far more appealing than the can of soda and sandwich with slices of pastrami piled high on rye bread sitting on his desk that he hadn't found the time yet to eat.

When he returned to his office, coffee in hand, he found Shipley waiting for him. The deputy had come to his office holding an incident report that didn't have any bearing on Abigail Wincoff's disappearance. But it was amongst the medley of other business the sheriff had to deal with on a regular basis.

He took a couple of gulps of his coffee and set the mug down on his desk. "So, what do you got for me, Deputy?"

Chapter 32

THAT MORNING of September 28 orders came from the head of the Pocono Mountain Regional Police Department in Pocono Summit that Detective Philip Silverwood had been assigned to the Abigail Wincoff case. Contributing reasons were that Andy Kirkman wasn't running for reelection for the office of county sheriff in November and the case just needed a fresh set of eyes. In addition, there was concern that Andy Kirkman was a bit rusty, which was chief among other issues brought to the attention of Philip Silverwood, with the utmost discretion.

His first task was to review the case file from the Monroe County Sheriff's Department, intent on poring over clues until he could unravel the mystery of how Abigail Wincoff vanished without an explanation. Then he was to re-interview Abigail's parents in New Jersey.

Closing his inner office door, Philip Silverwood dropped down into the chair behind his desk and steepled his fingers under his chin. Truth be told, he wasn't in the best mood, knowing he was going to have to meet with Andy Kirkman about the case, who he expected to be sensitive considering this was his last case as sheriff of Monroe County.

At thirty-six years old, Silverwood was a beefy fellow who had a square jaw filled with square white teeth, and a full head of brown hair. After graduating from high school, he had earned a degree in criminal justice from Ohio University. Subsequently, he joined the Pennsylvania State Police, was a street cop for four years, passed his exams and made sergeant, then promoted to detective at the age of twenty-nine. He'd always been guided by a sense of duty. And his dedication to the job was partly the reason he'd never been married, never had children, never been widowed.

Silverwood picked up his phone and dialed the seven familiar digits of the Monroe County Sheriff's Office, saying, "Sheriff Andy Kirkman," when the secretary came on the line.

"Who may I say is calling?"

"Detective Philip Silverwood of the Pocono Mountain Regional Police Department."

There was the sound of the call being transferred, then a man's voice: "Morning, Detective, what can I do you for?"

"Can I meet you at your office, tomorrow morning? I'd like to read the case file on the missing Abigail Wincoff. I've been assigned to investigate it. I'd like to hear your feedback. Questions? Theories?"

Taken aback by the sudden revelation, the sheriff's eyebrows knitted up so tight that they became one black line. The news was a blow to him. But, whatever his emotions, he maintained a professional self-control.

"Tomorrow morning's no problem," Kirkman said in a stern but shaky voice. "There's not much to tell and, there's not much to go on. In a nutshell, forensics found traces of her blood in the kitchen sink of the cabin on Wagon Trail Road. Outside, they found a partial footprint, but there is no guarantee that it's from the perp. Since the dogs had found nothing, divers dragged Meadow Lake looking for her for a week, but no body had been found. There aren't any witnesses. No sightings."

Silverwood was frowning. "The finding of her blood in the cabin is enough of an indication of an injury. In all likelihood she may have met a violent death."

"Let's hope not, but I must admit that very thought has crossed my mind many times," the sheriff stated with calm conviction.

The detective had participated in some high-profile cases, including missing child cases, all of which he had seen through to their happy or tragic outcomes. Something stirred inside of him. His brown eyes flickered as his thoughts wandered until he came to a disturbing conclusion. He knew from experience this was the work of a serial killer. It was cleverly planned and executed with barely a shred of evidence left behind.

"I'll share my hypothesis about how Abigail Wincoff died with you tomorrow."

"There's something else I want to say before you go. I've promised the girl's parents we're going to provide them some answers, and I'm determined to keep that promise. I hope I can count on you to work your hardest to make that happen," Kirkman said in a pleading way.

"I'll do my best. See you tomorrow, Andy."

The sheriff ended the call with mixed feelings. He leaned back in his seat, his chair screeching in protest. His opinion of Silverwood wasn't all that high. He sensed that Silverwood wasn't a bad sort, but he wasn't exactly a team player. More or less, Silverwood had a habit of being single-minded in his approach to his job as a detective. From past experience Kirkman knew the trouble that could bring. *Working with such a man*, Kirkman thought, *you might pick up the same habit.*

On the other hand, the sheriff respected Silverwood for his career experience, sterling ideas, and cool head under fire. He knew that Silverwood had been assigned the case mostly because of his proven track record in murder detection.

It was frustrating for Kirkman that he had no say in the matter. He wasn't content to play second string to the detective on the Abigail Wincoff case. But fretting about it wouldn't change a thing. With the election around the corner, and his impending retirement, he had to roll with the punches, but most importantly, hang on to his temper. Still, he would be in office until mid-January 2017, and he was determined to make the most of the time he had left to work with.

Chapter 33

ESTELLE ROWLAND had slept late on her day off, this last Thursday in September. It was nearly eleven. She sat up in the bed, snatched her glasses from the nightstand. Groggy from a dreamless sleep, she breathed in deep, her eyes adjusting to the sunlight that was streaming through the lace curtains as she looked around the room.

Curious about the weather, she peeked up at the sky from the small window of her mobile home. Soon enough the sun went under some clouds. Many of the clouds scattered across the sky were thick and others thin. However, it didn't look like it would rain. More than anything else she wanted to return to bed and stay there all day, but she couldn't avoid the fact that she had some important errands to run.

She left the window, took a shower then dressed in faded black jeans and an olive-green blouse that complemented her eyes.

Her stomach rumbled, reminding her that she hadn't eaten much of her dinner, and she'd slept through breakfast. So, she went to the kitchen to make herself some lunch. She put together a smoked turkey and provolone sandwich, added some apple slices, then took her plate to the table and sat down.

In no time, she'd finished her meal. After washing up, she went into the bedroom, gathered up her dirty clothes into a plastic laundry basket and set it on the bed. Then she opened a dresser drawer and pulled out a wad of ones and fives — her tip money from the past week. She stuffed the cash into an envelope and placed it in her handbag.

With a gleeful expression on her face, she closed the front door behind her and got into her Cadillac, drove out of the driveway, and headed toward the bank. Far from her mind was doing the laundry, her least-favorite thing. Not because it was a twenty-minute drive from her mobile home to the closest Laundromat in East Stroudsburg. Or because it usually took her two hours to get her laundry done. She had to stay there the whole time her clothes were in the machines because someone might steal them if she left. In principle, she felt her RV park should have a Laundromat on site and suggested it to the manager on a couple of occasions over the years.

Inside PNC Bank, she hummed along to the cheery music coming from the speaker in the ceiling above her as she filled out a deposit slip. Quickly afterward she greeted the teller and made the deposit. As she crossed the lobby on her way out, she waved to the bank manager sitting in a leather chair behind a large oak desk behind a low wooden railing.

Back in her car, the classic rock station on the radio came roaring to life. Stevie Nicks' throaty voice sang "Gypsy." The low beat of the music thrummed as she pulled out of the parking lot and turned onto Municipal Drive heading south, then made a left onto Milford Road.

After parking in the lot behind the facility, she shuffled out of the car carrying a plastic basket of dirty clothes. Just before reaching the entrance, she misstepped on the uneven ground, nearly tripping, but caught herself at the last moment.

The Coin-O-Matic Laundromat smelled of bleach and was blissfully empty except for a rather plump, orange-striped tabby cat sleeping on top of a dryer that had an out-of-order sign taped to it. Estelle was not fond of cats, but then she'd never had a pet as a child. Since her mother was allergic to animal hair, she never allowed animals in the house.

On the wall behind the washing machines, she noticed the sign with bold lettering. It informed customers to keep the Laundromat clean and not to over-sudsing the machine.

First, she put fifty cents in the vending machine for a little box of Arm & Hammer. Then she dumped her dirty clothes into the closest washing machine, added detergent, and turned the water temperature dial to warm. She inserted one dollars' worth of quarters and pushed the start button. Nothing happened. So, she bumped it with her hip and happily listened to the swish of the water.

The cat startled awake, meowed loudly, and gazed at her with its big yellow eyes. In turn, Estelle was startled. Then the cat jumped down from the top of the dryer, then found itself a hiding place scrunched in beside the drainpipe behind one of the washing machines. Probably Estelle scared the cat more than the cat scared her.

There was a cork bulletin board next to the dryers and she went over to read the notices. On the board, a Missing Child flyer of Abigail Wincoff surprised her. She read it, and then re-read it even though she'd seen it before. A duplicate copy was hanging in Victoria Station right now. But it had completely escaped her mind. She hadn't looked at it since the day the anchorwoman gave it to her.

Staring at Abby's photo, made her think of that day at the restaurant, the way that creep had been staring oddly at that little girl. She knew all too well that Abigail Wincoff was that little girl.

Estelle had yet to tell Sheriff Kirkman her suspicions, though. As far as she knew the sheriff hadn't come into the restaurant lately. She didn't want to go to the sheriff's office because she didn't have a crime to report. Even then, she was always tired after work. All she wanted to do was sit in her comfy wingback armchair and watch TV or nap after dinner.

Was it because she didn't want to look foolish to him? There was a chance she could be wrong about that creep.

She was still deciding how best to casually mention it next time she saw him. For certain she would say something. She wouldn't allow herself to forget.

Sometime later, Estelle was sitting in a row of chairs welded together, while her clothes were sudsing. She was engrossed in an article in an Architectural Digest magazine about designing living spaces that truly reflect your personality. When she flipped to the second page of the article, she found the page had been ripped out. In disgust, she flung the magazine aside.

At the sound of the magazine hitting the floor, the cat peeked out from behind a washing machine, watching her, and made a strange whimpering noise. It set Estelle's teeth on edge. As she saw its yellow eyes gleaming in the light and unnaturally still body, she just gave a whatever expression. The cat was scared, more than intimidated by Estelle's unwelcoming expression, and retreated into its hiding place behind the washing machine.

Chapter 34

AS THE SKY darkened, a waxing crescent moon was rising out of the spindly pine trees of a high ridge in the Pocono Mountains. The darkness reared up to cast its shadow over the cabin on Wagon Trail Road.

By a quarter past midnight, eerily, it was as if a cloud had passed over the moon, as the birds all stopped singing. The cabin appeared empty and deserted, desolate against the ink-black sky. The only light in the cabin was the moonglow filtering through the curtain-covered windows. The would-be novelist wasn't stirring about — not in any physical sense, that is — but she seemed not to be there at all. Perhaps Gail was sleeping in one of the bedrooms.

The thump of a door being unbraced, and a squeak of hinges interrupted the silence. Soft footsteps echoed down the hall. The pull-down attic stairs started creaking like the hull of an old ship. And lastly, a faint noise inside the attic.

Creaking floorboards. Someone was there … an unwelcome guest, judging by the sounds.

The moon through the small, circular window cast a soft glow on the culprit of the noises that was sitting on the dusty wood floor of the attic. The ghost of Abby had her eyes fixed on the doll, cradled in her arms.

For no apparent reason, she shook the doll forcefully, hesitated a second, rocked it and whispered to it. "Down came the Good Fairy, and she said, "Little Bunny Foo Foo, I don't like your attitude."

Giggling, she lowered the doll to the floor between her legs. Using a long, sharp fingernail, she slit its belly packed tight with cotton. Violently, she pulled the stuffing out and out, and she giggled some more.

The television on the top of a rectangular, wooden table in the corner of the room, was going haywire — first with ragged gray static and then with violent zigzagging lines on the screen. Abby's ghost took her blank, dark eyes off the doll and cast a glance at the gritty television garbled with static and lines.

In those few seconds, a large crow with faded, ruffled wings had landed with an ominous caw on the outer sill. The solitary crow could see Abby's ghost and stared at her with eyes that were eerily sentient. She cast a glance at it. The bird didn't fly away. It answered with several pecks on the window, then continued to stare. Then, the crow cocked its head sideways, warbling a throaty caw before it pecked lightly at the window again. Tap, tap, tap.

Hastily averting her glance, Abby disregarded the crow. She rose from the floor and watched the static dance on the screen, seemingly entranced, whispering inaudible words. Her white dress shimmered in the unnatural glow of the television's static. The torn-up doll, dressed in a red polka dot dress, hung loosely in her hand.

Transfixed, she stepped closer to the television screen, and the doll slipped from her fingers, landing on the floor. Staring intensely at the television burbling with silent static before her, she proceeded to climb into it. Soon afterward, her ghostly face appeared on the static-filled television screen. Gradually, Abby's spirit manifested itself into the static.

In short, the television served as a portal, or conduit, to the realm of the dead. And there was nothing to fill the silence but the static from the television. Not until the crow on the windowsill cawed loudly. Then it abruptly flew away into the trees.

Just before the television went off, Abby's voice cried out through static-laden television transmission. "Help me, help me."

Hours later, when the sun rose, the cabin itself seemed to have stopped breathing. There were no more creaks or shudders in the floorboards. At that time, Gail woke up on the couch. She'd slept there all night in the same clothes she was wearing yesterday. A pink cardigan over a short-sleeved white blouse dotted with pink and red flowers, and tan slacks. She'd been working around the clock to finish her book, napping during breaks on the couch, sometimes twice a day.

Pale sunlight filtered through the curtains, slanting across the beige walls, and giving the room a cozy intimacy. She looked at the old clock on the fireplace mantel. It was half past seven.

A powerful surge of emotions swelled in her. Suddenly, she had a flash of a memory from when she was a child. Twelve years old. A time in her life when she was always bubbling with laughter and joy. It reminded her of the dream she had last night. In that dream, she had been in the backseat of her parents' vehicle singing a song to her doll. She could see her mother clearly then, that natural way she had of making her feel comfortable, her sparkling eyes watching her in the rearview mirror. She used to love to sing. In particular she liked nursery rhymes. On several occasions, she had sung to her mother and her father too. Until this very moment, she had never before realized just how much she missed her parents, who were gone from her now.

A deep breath shuddered in her chest, overwhelmed by all the emotions swamping her. She closed her eyes in order to strengthen herself and compose her thoughts. When she opened her eyes and sat up, her mind was on her novel. She looked at the typewriter on the side table for a long time. And then she sat down in front of the typewriter and put a sheet of paper through the roller. She wrung her hands tightly, staring at the blank paper protruding from the typewriter, and started tapping away at the keys.

Outside the cabin, the sky was a perfect, cloudless blue. The sun was shining brightly on this third day of October. Angling in from the east, its warm rays shining down on what was looking like a pleasant autumn day. It only seemed fitting that for this year's All Hallows Eve Abby's ghost would be lurking around.

Chapter 35

AT THE TIME Gail, the author, was staying in the cabin that Abigail Wincoff's ghost was haunting, the Detective from the Pocono Mountain Regional Police Department assigned to her case was paying a visit to her parents' sprawling two-story home.

On a Saturday afternoon in early October, Detective Philip Silverwood stepped out of the department-issued Chevrolet Tahoe and shut the driver's door with a slam that seemed to echo in the quiet of Timberline Way. He stood on the cracked concrete sidewalk, and his cop's eyes scanned the neighborhood, right to left and back the other way. All the houses were well-kept, gardens with neatly trimmed hedges, and flower beds on the manicured green lawns.

Not a second too soon, Silverwood stepped up on the porch and noticed the bird feeder, full of seed. He lifted the heavy brass knocker on the front door. Within seconds, he heard a faint shuffle of footsteps approaching and the door swung open almost before he let go of the knocker.

"Good afternoon. My name is Philip Silverwood. I'm with the Criminal Investigation Unit of the Pocono Mountain Regional Police Department. May I come in, to talk with you?"

"I suppose this is about Abby?" Lance Wincoff asked, lips hardly moving. "I wish you'd called ahead."

He sounded like one of those ventriloquist acts where a guy made his performing dummy look as if it were talking.

"Yes, I should have. I apologize for not doing that," Silverwood replied.

"Please come in," he said formally, then stepped back as Silverwood entered the house and went into the living room. "Can I make you some coffee or something?"

The detective ignored his offering and simply asked, "Can we sit?"

When Gillian came into the room and sat on one end of sofa next to her husband, Silverwood sat down on the loveseat. The Wincoffs both looked a mess. She hadn't been eating much lately; the appetite just wasn't there. She was simply grieving. The dark circles under her brown eyes, and rumpled clothes that were clean, but ill-fitting; suggested a woman getting through the day as best she could. Lance looked disheveled and only half awake, lines of fatigue etched around his eyes. His wrinkled, white shirt hung out of his olive-green khaki pants. For her parents,

Abby's absence felt wrong, as if a piece of them had been cut away.

"I'll be fast. I know this must be a tough time for you," Silverwood said, as if thinking aloud.

"Did you come here to tell me to stop bugging Sheriff Kirkman?" She choked and broke off, staring down at the floor for a few seconds to gather her strength, then looked up at Silverwood.

Gillian had called the Monroe County Sheriff's Office too many times, irritating the police, which might make them turn against her. But she desperately wanted to know what the police were doing to find Abby. She focused her glare on him but said nothing more and waited for his explanation.

"I wouldn't put it like that," the detective said.

"I know I've been calling a lot. I want to know what happened to my daughter. It's just that this has been a stressful time for me," she said, then fell silent, looking around the room.

Were they telling the truth about how their daughter went missing? The suspicion nagged at the detective, then wavered. On the surface, he felt they were, in fact, grieving parents.

"Understandable," Silverwood said. "To all intents and purposes, we're actively investigating all leads. But there's so much we don't know."

Once upon a time, when Philip Silverwood was first hired by the department, being promoted to the Criminal Investigation Unit felt like an honor. Now, after nearly thirteen years on the force, nothing shocked or fazed him. Sadly, just like so many other cases, he wondered if he could find justice for this victim, Abigail Wincoff, who he believed had been murdered.

Gillian shook her head, sighed, and opened her mouth to speak, but her husband cut in. "How can we help?"

"Did you hear any unusual sounds that morning your daughter disappeared?" the detective asked her.

Suddenly Gillian was shaking. She cupped her hands underneath her elbows and hugged herself tight, trying to suppress her shaking.

She rolled her eyes, trying to remember. "That Tuesday morning in mid-August, I didn't hear or see anything out of the ordinary."

"I just had to ask," said the detective, his eyes watching her thoughtfully.

Silverwood asked questions to clarify situations. She recounted as much as she could remember of the moment, she discovered her daughter was missing.

The detective let it all sink in, turned to Lance and asked, "Is there any reason to think someone might have snatched your daughter?"

"There is no reason that I know of," Lance answered, dumbfounded.

"The way I see it is that the perp was watching and waiting outside the cabin for a chance to snatch her. For whatever reason, your daughter went into the woods. And he saw his opportunity," said the detective, rising to his feet.

Detective Silverwood pulled a business card out of his wallet and handed it to Gillian. "That has my contact information on it. I'll try my best to get you some answers."

She nodded, then tucked the card in her jeans pocket.

"From this point on, we'll be treating this as a murder investigation," Silverwood said to both of them.

The sad truth that the detective needed to say, and they needed to hear him say it.

"But there's no body," Lance said with resolution and stood up.

"Mr. Wincoff," the detective said with a heavy sigh, "Given the violence implied by the blood we have found, we have to work with the assumption that Abigail has been murdered."

Lance thought about what the detective had just said, tried to digest the words.

Gillian Wincoff wasn't listening any longer. Starting to go teary-eyed, she pulled her knees into her body. She hugged herself tightly, rocking slowly back and forth. The detective and her husband hadn't seemed to notice this. But then her hand trembled as she put it on the armrest to support herself as she abruptly stood up and left the room without a word.

Lance called after her, but no, she was resolute. She did not return. Instead, she ran up the stairs and slammed a door. Then he made an attempt at normal conversation.

"The truth may be a terrible thing to accept, but I believe not knowing is worse for my wife than the truth. She's upset — that's understandable, right?"

"Perfectly," Silverwood said and made a move for the door.

The well-meaning detective gave Lance a handshake like a grip of iron. "For what it's worth, even if we don't find her body, I have no doubt her killer will be caught. Maybe not today, or tomorrow, but someday."

"I trust the police to find out what happened to Abby," Lance said, before closing the door behind him.

When Lance turned back to the living room, he was silent, too despondent, and tormented, and too macho to reach out to his wife. He wasn't going to let himself cry in front of her, so he headed toward his home office.

Chapter 36

ONCE GILLIAN WINCOFF had heard the door close downstairs, she leaned back against the door of her daughter's bedroom. Her grief was so dense that she felt as though she couldn't draw a breath, almost as if her lungs had forgotten how to work in concert. At last, a long-ragged breath escaped her chest. But her heart was still flapping like a panicked bird. This couldn't be happening. Had she lost Abby for good? Ever since she vanished, she felt as if a part of her had vanished too, and she'd been struggling to come to terms with what had happened to her. Now the only hope she had of her daughter returning had been snuffed out of her the moment Detective Philip Silverwood so bluntly put it, "Abigail has been murdered."

As she turned around to face the door; for the first time she grudgingly admitted to herself that the detective had a point about the evidence pointing to her daughter's death.

What was Abby's blood doing in the kitchen sink of another cabin in East Stroudsburg?

Maybe it was time for her to face the music — Abby was dead.

Gillian opened the door to Abby's room. Something she hadn't done since her disappearance.

She sank into a delicate lavender velvet-cushioned chair beside her daughter's twin bed with a quilt yanked over the scrunched-up sheets. That was the way Abby had left it before leaving for the Poconos. Slowly, she let her eyes wander around the room. Her wooden four-drawer dresser was piled with coloring books, crayons, and littered with Barbie dolls and their paraphernalia. The walls were plastered with pictures of Belle, the Beast, Cinderella and Snow White. In the corner stood a bookcase filled with books, and a little pile of books sat on her bedside table with bookmarks sticking out.

The painful transition from life-with-Abby to life-without-Abby was upon her. On more than one occasion she and Lance had discussed having another child. It was something they'd planned to do since Abby had turned ten, but now things were not right. She felt a little ashamed of having let such a thought cross her mind.

She opened the double doors of her closet and took in the mess. Time and time again, she had told Abby to gather up the stuffed animals and clothes from around the room. She frowned when she saw that Abby had tossed everything that had been on the floor or on her bed into her closet.

"I love you, Abby," she said gently, wishing she could wrap her arms around Abby and give her a hug.

As she touched some of the hanging clothes, she felt it then — felt the tears trembling at the corners of her eyes. Crying quietly, she drew in a shuddering breath. All this time, she'd been angry with herself for not waking up sooner, for taking a nap in the first place. Had she indeed endangered her child by leaving her unattended for almost ninety minutes in a cabin? She sighed deeply. The frustration was weighing down on her.

A sudden burst of laughter drifted into the room to shatter the silence. A family with three little girls lived in the house across the road. She could hear the girls laughing and playing behind their house where there was a jungle gym and swing set. The sound of the little girls' laughter screeched across her peace of mind like fingernails on a chalkboard. It was too much for her broken heart. Unable to bear it any longer, she left the room. She hurried down the bedroom-wing hallway and retreated to a quiet part of the house.

An hour later the brass door knocker sounded. Lance Wincoff hustled to the front door and found Louise Melinda Sisler waiting on the porch. She was dressed in a cashmere sweater and wool slacks, and her graying hair loose about her shoulders. This was her fourth visit to the house since their return from the Poconos, and Lance knew, whether he approved or not, that his wife needed her.

"Mrs. Sisler, it's a pleasure to see you," he greeted his mother-in-law.

She mustered up a smile. "Thank you, Lance. Got a late start this morning, but I'm here to help now. Where is she?"

"She's upstairs in the bedroom, I think."

"I hope you don't mind getting my luggage out of the car," she said in a sweet tone and indicated her suitcase with a wave of her hand as she stepped inside. "I'm late as it is."

Gillian's mother lived on Mill Road in Morris Plains, New Jersey in a small three-bedroom pitched-roof house with a pair of conjoined trees in the front yard. The branches and trunks of the old trees had curled, and then grafted together. For her, the world had always been simple and sane. She'd loved her husband, Bruce, and her two daughters, tended a garden, and sang in the choir at her church. But nothing serious happened to change her routine until her husband died suddenly.

Lately, she found it difficult to adapt to life as a widow. In the two years since the passing of her husband, Louise found spending time with her daughters comforting and went a long way toward filling the void. It was her way of coping. Yet now, with Abby's disappearance, coupled with her youngest daughter, Carolyn, in the process of a messy divorce, made her two daughters equally vulnerable. They needed her. And it was a good feeling to be needed. It gave her a sense of purpose and tugged at her maternal instincts.

So that night Gillian and her mother talked in the living room until around two in the morning. By the time she joined Lance in the bedroom he was fast asleep. She put on her nightgown and got into bed. After some tossing and turning, she fell asleep, the blanket pulled up to her chin.

The next morning, Lance had woken up at seven a.m. He turned onto his side and watched his wife breathing against the pillow. His beautiful wife. He placed his hand against her cheek, smoothed her hair back from her face, and kissed her forehead. Sometimes he wished she could talk to him without that worried look of hers, the way she'd been ever since Abby's disappearance. With that thought in mind, he left the bed, snatched his robe off the hook on the back of the bathroom door. He slipped it on and tied the belt as he walked out of the room.

Chapter 37

THAT SAME Sunday morning Sheriff Andy Kirkman was relaxing on the sofa in the living room of his two-story, four-bedroom, three-and-a-half-bath colonial house on Bryant Street in Stroudsburg. He was idly flicking through the paper, working his way to the sports pages. In the quiet room, he could hear the rain outside, a furious, driving rain, and the steady plink of the drops as they blew against the window.

But the thought of rain reminded him of the futile search for Abigail Wincoff last August. Until the Abigail Wincoff case fell into his lap, his work in the past few months had required him to spend more time doing paperwork at a desk. This was perfectly logical since he was not running for reelection for the office of county sheriff. But leaving the case unsolved with a multitude of questions unanswered wasn't how he wanted to retire. And the fact that this was really no longer his case depressed him.

He folded up the newspaper, placed it on the mahogany coffee table in front of the sofa, and punched the remote on the television to watch NBC. His favorite pastime was to watch a Philadelphia Eagles football game — not without dozing off from time to time — as most men did when they watched sports alone. At the end of the first quarter, his head was nodding from side to side as if he might fall asleep at any moment.

His wife, Merrilee, strolled into the living room and noticed him napping. She smiled to herself, then picked up the remote lying next to him on the sofa and turned off the flat-screen TV. She headed into the kitchen to make lunch.

At home, the sheriff was just Andy Kirkman, laid back and down-to-earth. Over the years, she had learned what it meant to be the wife of a sheriff. Though she undoubtedly didn't fit the stereotype because she was short and thin, frail-looking and had a soft voice. What she found particularly hardest to cope with was his long hours on the job. On more occasions than she could count, she had left his dinner plate covered in aluminum foil on the kitchen table. Soon to be the wife of a retired sheriff, she looked forward to sit-down dinners around the table and little vacations for the two of them.

At around 11:30, Andy Kirkman woke up to delicious smells coming from the kitchen. It was already lunchtime. In one movement he came off the sofa and made his way into a spacious kitchen. There were white, sheer curtains around two big windows with a partial view of the backyard. He took a seat in one of the chairs at the small, round table with a brooding look on his face. And Merrilee caught it.

"What's with the frown?" she asked before turning back to the oven.

"Retirement sucks," he grumbled.

"Is that so?" she asked with her back turned to him.

His eyes narrowed, causing them to crinkle at the corners, the way they always did when he smiled. "My biggest concern is that I'll be so bored I could gouge out my eyes."

She knew he was feeling miserable because he had so far failed to solve his last case. So, she didn't press him and kept the conversation light, steering it in another direction.

"I think I know where this is leading. You've changed your mind? You're going to run for reelection?" she asked, in a teasing way. "After all, you're still young."

They had often teased each other about such things which kept the two of them on their toes. Like most marriages, theirs could get very dull sometimes, dominated by routine.

"No, I haven't changed my mind. I'm going to step down. Honestly, I've been feeling burnt out lately. Plus, you know, I joined the force young and had planned to retire young."

"So then tell me dear. What's all the angst about?" she asked in a concerned wifely voice.

"Try not to take it personally. Because I really want to be with you twenty-four-seven and spend our golden years together. It's just that retiring with my last case unsolved leaves a bitter taste in my mouth," he said, then sighed.

The oven timer dinged, and she pulled out the pan from the oven. The scent of chicken, tomato and spices filled the air as she placed it on the kitchen counter.

"This will fix you right up. Fresh from the oven. My late mother's chicken cacciatore recipe usually does the trick with you."

"I don't disagree. Right now, a delicious meal will be perfect," he added with a smile and a wink.

Seeing his smile, his spirits uplifted, in response, she couldn't help but smile too, knowing how happy that made her.

When his daughter Kara came into the kitchen, he gave her a questioning glance but nodded before she took a seat at the table. She had her arms folded over her chest, a cute pout on her face. Though she was tall, she had an average build for a fourteen-year-old. She wore black lipstick, black nail polish and black combat boots to go with her baggy jeans and cut-off T-shirt, that didn't quite cover her belly button. Aside from her taste in fashion, to her parents, she was the joy of their lives.

Kara glanced up with a smile when her mother set a plate in front of her. "Smells good, Mom."

Merrilee untied her apron and hung it on its designated hook on the wall. As she joined them at the table, she thought how lucky she was to have him as her husband. As well as being handsome, with strong features, he was also kind, and considerate. Today was one of those days she was simply cherishing her time with him and her daughter. She took a sip of her sparkling water, then began to eat.

Chapter 38

DETECTIVE SILVERWOOD parked his Tahoe in the driveway of the chestnut log cabin off Sellersville Drive in East Stroudsburg, the last place Abigail Wincoff had been seen before she had disappeared. It was after ten o'clock on a Monday morning. He grabbed a 7-Eleven cup of coffee from a drink holder and chugged. His thoughts were on the Wincoffs, whom he had seen the day before in their New Jersey home. He really felt bad for them but was even more upset by the inadequacy of the case and lack of evidence thereof. To top it off, he had a stubborn sheriff to deal with. Andy Kirkman didn't want to leave the case unsolved, even if it wasn't going to be his case anymore. Silverwood smiled to himself at the thought of a new sheriff. And he was sort of looking forward to it.

All in all, Silverwood was a different sort of officer from Kirkman, which he knew from first-hand experience.

The two had butted heads during a hit-and-run case, though he'd been gracious enough to acknowledge the detective's contribution to its resolution. He believed Andy Kirkman wasn't the sharpest tool in the shed. But he had to admit Kirkman had good people skills, his mind was naturally analytic, and he was fiercely loyal to his community. Whereas he himself, wasn't a community-minded man, but rather lived for his detective work, had few close friends and few outside interests.

The detective set his coffee into the drink holder and skittered away from his thoughts. He got out of his car and immediately studied the area around the cabin. Tipped his head slightly, listened intently, and tried to think like the perp. The killer in waiting would have sought out spots to watch the cabin without being seen, in all probability behind a tree, and there were lots of them.

Next, the detective walked through the woods in the direction he thought Abigail Wincoff might have chosen to go. Then he stopped at the location where the binoculars belonging to Abby had been found, took out his notepad, and started making some notes.

The cabin on Wagon Trail Road was the last place he wanted to visit. To get there, he took the simplest route, thinking the perp would have taken a short cut. He also believed the perp had washed Abigail Wincoff's blood off himself in the kitchen sink. The forensics team couldn't find any traces of a struggle. There was no blood, nothing to indicate that she'd been harmed in the cabin. There was nothing that proved that she had been in there. They also examined the ground around the cabin as well as the land around it, but nothing had been found.

From the forest's edge he had a clear view of the cabin. The first thing he noticed about the cabin was that it had an empty air. He stopped to survey the surroundings and took a deep breath. There was no smell of decaying flesh from the area. But there was an eerie silence in the surrounding woods. That was until he heard the flutter of wings above his head. A crow swooped out of the trees and flew to the roof of the cabin. It tilted its head to one side and looked at him.

"Caw, caw, caw."

"Shhh!" Silverwood hissed at the crow.

By the time he'd made a full circle around the cabin, examining the ground for good measure, the crow was no longer on the roof. Based on his observations, he could see that everything was as it should be. So, it was reasonable for the detective to believe that Abigail Wincoff was killed and buried somewhere else. He pulled out his notepad from his inner jacket pocket and jotted down some notes.

Turning to head back into the woods, he heard running footsteps and a little girl's giggle. He darted a glance in the direction of the sounds and saw what looked like a girl in a white dress, resembling Abigail Wincoff's description.

"Abby," the detective called out from the distance. "Abigail Wincoff."

The running figure of a girl stopped and wrenched her head in his direction. He could sort of see her marble white face. The pupils of her eyes were black and staring. In her hand she was clutching a doll. She was trembling violently.

"I'm Detective Philip Silverwood, Pocono Mountain Regional PD," he said. "Are you Abigail Wincoff?"

He needed to ask. Somewhere deep in his subconscious he wanted her to be there. And he wasn't surprised by that revelation. He wished he could find Abigail. But he was certain in his gut that she was dead. And he didn't want her to be dead.

Who was he looking at?

A loud piercing caw with a deep shrill startled him. Silverwood turned his head toward the sound. He then looked back at the little girl. The crow was right where the little girl had been standing, staring at him. Then, suddenly, the crow flew off languidly without a second look in his direction.

Before he could walk over there, he caught a glimpse of the girl running in another part of the woods. The detective started running after her. But after rounding some trees, he lost sight of her and found himself staring directly at the cabin off Sellersville Drive, where his Tahoe was parked in the driveway.

A moment later, he heard whispering behind him. A trill of giggles. Turning to look in every possible direction, the little girl was nowhere to be seen.

The detective faced the woods and called out, "Abigail Wincoff."

As the detective stood at the edge of the woods, panting, trying to catch his breath, his mind was trying to understand what had just happened. Did he really see a little girl? Abigail Wincoff?

His eyes studied the area before he speculated aloud, "Her bare feet would've left footprints in the dirt. Nothing. There aren't any footprints."

His stomach growled. And he concluded that mere coffee wasn't enough for this morning. Perhaps too much caffeine on an empty stomach caused him to hallucinate. And he felt foolish for chasing after a ghost. Not a real ghost, but a ghost in his mind's eye. Had to be. He was a very logical man, and he couldn't come up with any other explanation.

As the detective climbed into his Tahoe and pulled out of the driveway, it was no longer relevant to him whether he saw something or not. He just wanted to forget the incident ever happened.

On his way to lunch, he stopped at a Gulf station to have his SUV gassed up. Then he ran it through the car wash to get rid of the layer of fine brown dust covering the vehicles that made trips up and down the dirt roads that led to the rental cabins in the Poconos.

Chapter 39

LATE ON A MONDAY AFTERNOON, Kristi Maratos walked into the Eastern Monroe Public Library to research a story she was working on. Luckily, she discovered early in her television journalism career that if you want to get ahead, you had better know your stuff.

The clerk behind the circulation didn't even look up when she passed. For a brief moment, she glimpsed the sign with arrows that directed library patrons to various sections. She came to a complete stop when she saw Billy Shipley sitting at one of the tables. The deputy was off duty, reading a book and taking notes.

In a fleeting moment, she decided she would approach him after she found a book for her research. She did not want to look eager to see him. Were other women drawn to him the way she was? With his good looks, he could be intimidating to any single woman. Not that, God forbid, she was on the lookout for Mr. Right.

Later, when she approached the table, he looked up to see her. He smiled as he gestured for her to sit.

"Good afternoon, Deputy. Kristi Maratos television news," she said comically.

His eyes met hers. "I remember you."

"I'll just sit for a minute. I don't want to interrupt your reading," she said humbly.

His eyes remained locked on her. "It's no bother at all. I could use a break after studying all morning. I'm working on my master's degree in public administration at East Stroudsburg University."

Kristi met his gaze with an answering smile. "How fascinating. I'm just here collecting information on a developing news story."

"What's it about? If you don't mind me asking, that is," Shipley asked with a curious expression on his face.

"Changes in wildlife populations over the years due to the influx of tourism. There are less white tail deer in this area than there was twenty years ago. Wildlife and tourism don't go together. As much as we'd like to believe they do, the facts are the facts."

He smiled widely at her. "I'd like to hear more. Maybe you could tell me about it over dinner sometime."

His smile closed up instantly. And she liked that he had surprised himself with the invitation. Clearly, he sort of enjoyed watching the blush work its way up from her neck up to her cheekbones.

"Are you asking me out? Like a date or something?" she asked purposely looking deeper into his eyes.

Shipley ran a hand through his hair, looked down at the tabletop, then back at her again with a new intensity in his eyes. "Well, I just meant conversation and a bite to eat. But if it was a date. Would I be out of line to ask?"

In that moment she liked the way he was looking at her, the timid look in his eyes. It made her feel like a teenager again — a teenager head over heels.

Kristi didn't hesitate. "Where did you have in mind to go for a bite to eat?"

"There's a good place about two blocks from here. Just follow my car," he said, and closed his book with a snap.

They met in the parking lot of Raffles Bistro on 9th Street. It was an all-night restaurant serving moderately expensive American regional cuisine. The clientele was local, as opposed to tourists. And it was a popular haunt with police officers both on and off duty. The owner, a sixtyish Armenian guy named Gregor appreciated it when they stopped in for a meal or coffee. Their presence during the late hours, he said, kept bad guys away.

Billy Shipley had been coming to this hole-in-the-wall greasy spoon for most of his short career, which would span four years this month. He found the food and casual atmosphere just the right combination.

"Sad about that little girl, Abigail something. I seemed to have forgotten her last name. Do you think there's any chance of finding her?" she asked casually, without looking up from her cold pasta salad.

"Over two months since she disappeared, and police are no closer to finding her," he frowned as he rubbed the back of his head.

"I felt bad that day, reporting from outside the cabin knowing her parents were inside," Kristi said, before taking another bite of her salad.

"That was a stressful time for me. I was working around-the-clock searching the woods for her."

"I can just imagine," she said, munching thoughtfully.

"Though I must admit that something good happened that day," Shipley said with a suspicious grin and a sexy twitch of his mustache.

"What was that?" she asked, rather surprised.

"I met you that day. Remember?"

"You don't need to remind me. I'm glad you think it was good meeting me," she said with a laugh, which he took as a good sign.

"Now that I said that I feel kind of funny," he admitted with a grin.

"Why is that?"

Shipley leaned back into the booth's seat cushion. "I'm wondering if you think it's too soon to say something like that."

"Here we are, having a casual meal together," she reminded him. "I'll simply point out that we're obviously attracted to each other."

"Good point," Shipley said, then sat forward, picked up his knife and fork and cut off a slice of his steak.

"Do you think Abigail is dead?" she returned the subject back.

"I'm not at liberty to discuss the case. I can only state the obvious, that she can't be found."

"The reporter in me just couldn't help but bring it up," Kristi said, and returned to her meal.

Chapter 40

AT 9:10 on that particular Wednesday morning in October, Gail sat at the typewriter completely engrossed in her manuscript. Unbeknownst to her, the ghost of Abigail Wincoff still lurked around the cabin.

The noisy clacking sound of the typewriter filtered out from the living room. The clack-clack-clack of the keys hitting the paper rang out like gunshots. Abruptly, the typewriter fell silent for a good long while, and then burst into life for a minute.

When Gail paused to read the last paragraph, she had typed, she thought she heard a little girl's voice from outside the cabin. She didn't want to look out the window. Instead, she waited three minutes, listening for voices, but didn't hear anything. Not that she really cared anyway. These days she only cared about one thing. Writing her book.

What seemed like mere minutes later, a voice came through a vent in the ceiling. A heating and cooling vent that led to the attic.

A little girl's voice said, "Please come and play with me. I'm so lonely."

Gail only caught a faint sound, and briefly looked up. When she didn't hear anything again, she began to tap on the keys.

"Safe in the peaceful surroundings," she said and typed, "she went deeper into the woods. From a distance there was a dangerous madman watching her, lurking in the shadows of the trees."

The little girl's voice came softer than before. "I don't want to play alone."

She'd been so engrossed in her work and lost in the world she was creating. She failed to hear it or respond to it.

Squinting a little as she typed away feverishly, she didn't notice Abby's transparent figure slowly materialize up near the ceiling. The room had grown suddenly cooler. Something decaying, the smell of something rotten filled Gail's nose, and forced her to look toward the ceiling. Just in the corner, floated the ghost of Abigail Wincoff — as still as death — her chalk-white face, shrouded in shadow. In disbelief, Gail tensed.

Gazing down at her from the ceiling, Gail felt Abby's intense gaze penetrating deeply into her soul. In response, she tried to scream, but the only sound she made was a soft gasp.

Finally, she pushed off her chair with all her might and stood. She backed up, knees trembling, her breath whistling softly in and out of her. With waves of dread building inside her, she plastered her back against the wall beside the couch.

Gail was cornered, standing motionless at the foot of the white suede couch … waiting. Tension mounted. With each passing minute, her eyes had grown wider, and she'd unconsciously moved closer to the couch.

Abby's ghost floated down from the ceiling and hovered right in front of her, staring intently. Gail squeezed her eyes tightly shut. What she didn't see was that Abby's spirit began to backpedal slowly. Never turning her back to Gail, she opened the hallway closet door, and disappeared inside.

Her anxiety building, Gail could stand it no longer. Taking a deep breath, she forced herself to open her eyes. She had half convinced herself that when she did, the ghost would be standing before her. But the room was empty.

Still, she felt watched.

Her face was a mask of horror. Fear had left her vulnerable and weak. She collapsed on the couch breathing heavily.

A ghostly voice disturbed the quiet of the room. A little girl, giggling, complete with long pauses of silence in between to resettle. And then a ghostly screech, louder than any sound Gail had heard so far, echoed through the space around her. The dreadful piercing noise cut through her head like a chainsaw, making her close her eyes. It was only when she opened them again, she saw nothing but blurry shapes. After a little shake of her head, she closed them again.

Then Abby spoke, "Can you help me find Carrie? I want my doll. I lost her. Please help me find her."

Gail sensed a presence. Turning her head to look behind her, she saw the shadow of an arm with a claw-like hand on the wall reaching down toward her head. Terrified, she let out a little shriek. In a single motion she curled herself up into a fetal position. She looked as if she was part of the couch, head pushed back into the cushion.

Abby began to sing. "Ring around the rosy, pocket full of posies, ashes, ashes, we all fall down."

The singing got louder and louder. Gail found it more and more difficult to tolerate. Instinctively she raised her hands to her ears, covering them. With her eyes closed tightly, Gail began to hum in her mind. It was a desperate attempt to distract herself from the unyielding sounds she could not bear.

In one fell swoop, the singing stopped. Where had Abby's ghost gone to? Hearing nothing for many minutes, Gail reopened her eyes. She lay still and silent, her unfocused eyes staring blankly at nothing.

A high-pitched scream pierced the air — loud enough that it could be heard outside the cabin. Whimpering sobs and shivering sighs followed the outburst. The sound of a voice crying out made her tremble. Gail pulled the hood of her pink cardigan over her head to drown out the noise.

At long last Abby ended with a bone-chilling howl that turned into a scream. For the next ninety minutes, there was complete silence. But still, Gail was terrified. Somehow the silence was worse than the menacing voice could have been.

Fear had drained her strength. After a short interval collecting herself, she twisted her body into a relaxed position on the couch. One of her hands was tucked under the cheek, the other was splayed on her cardigan-covered stomach. She began to drift off to sleep.

Chapter 41

THE GHOST of Abigail Wincoff was lurking around the cabin in the wee hours of the morning. Faint moaning filled the air as she manifested herself in the living room, followed by a hushed silence. She moved in a ghostly glide across the room to the table where the typewriter sat. While in that spot, she cast her eyes down at the unfinished manuscript. For a period of time, she stared at it, as if gazing into the abyss.

As if sensing something, Abby turned her eyes toward the couch, where Gail was sleeping. She moved toward the couch, her feet barely touching the floor. She stopped a foot away, taking everything in with a brief glance before she turned to face Gail. A giggle escaped her, and she clapped her hand over her mouth, as if she didn't want to wake her. But then she sang to her.

"Little Bunny Foo Foo. Hopping through the forest."

Gail didn't stir. She was sleeping curled up like a baby, her back deep into the cushions.

It would soon be daylight. Abby made some whispering sounds, then moved to the center of the living room. She turned and disappeared down the hallway.

At this time Gail was in a deep sleep, in the middle of an early morning nightmare from which she couldn't wake up. Images of the ghost, of birds, of the moon and blood played through her unconscious, making her twitch as she slept.

The bad dream began with her leaving the cabin. In the twilight hours she set off through a meadow of spiky weeds and wildflowers on her way to the woods. When she looked over her shoulder, she saw the ghost in the attic window. Without shifting her gaze from the ghostly girl, she quickened her pace, her mind racing with thoughts of escape.

The ghostly voice called through the window, "Come and play with me."

The voice was low, almost hypnotizing, and a second later the ghost of the little girl vanished. The square of light in the window slowly faded away to darkness. The cabin darkened. Everything darkened around her. She turned her eyes forward, walking faster.

Gail entered the woods, where a symphony of crickets pulsed and pulsed. She gazed at a big maple tree. Moonlight shone through its branches casting shadows everywhere that she couldn't tell where she was, or when.

"Here in the forest, dark and deep," came the ghostly voice.

Ignoring the voice, she raised her binoculars and spotted a pileated woodpecker just before it flew off. She started following it. Jumping over a downed log, she sprinted as she chased the bird determined not to lose sight of it.

The pileated woodpecker landed on a branch of a pine tree and began to preen its tail. She stopped and raised her binoculars to view it. It stopped preening its tail feathers, tucked his head down and retracted its tail between his legs. For a split second the bird's eyes flashed red when it lifted its head and started pecking away at the bark of the tree.

Without warning, the pileated woodpecker took off, swooped and dived into the trees and out of sight. With a disappointed sigh at the bleak darkness of her surroundings, she lowered the binoculars.

Gail was alone in the woods, feeling lost and alone. Her mind spinning in and out of dark places. Hands trembling, she clutched the binoculars to her chest. All she heard were the sounds — insects, birds, and other animals she couldn't see screeched, and buzzed, chattering to one another.

"Little Bunny Foo Foo. Hopping through the forest. Scooping up the field mice," came the ghostly voice again.

Panting with terror, her only thought was to run away. That she did.

She didn't get far — she hadn't been running for long when she caught a glimpse through the trees of a ghostly figure of a little girl running. Then something knocked her to the ground. She tried to get up, looked at her clothes and noticed she was wearing a white dress. It was as if she had become someone else entirely, someone smaller and much weaker than herself.

Something pushed her down again. The sudden blow made her head spin. She clamped her eyes shut, fighting the nausea.

The presence of evil was all around her. Despite her weak state, she was acutely aware of it. She heaved a shaky sigh as she dug her fists into the ground, trying to raise herself up enough so that she could see who was doing this to her. But there was only a dark shape, a shadow among shadows.

Another blow — harder than the last one, then down on the ground again. She couldn't move. Her arms didn't seem to belong to her. A low moan rumbled up from deep in her chest. Why was this happening to her? What had she done wrong? Who would want to hurt her?

The questions tumbled about in her mind, but no answers came to her.

A brilliant, intense white light descended from the dark sky, hovering right in front of her face. And then, in a sudden shift, she felt loved.

Why was it there?

Her squinting eyes stared into the light. She couldn't seem to look away. The longer she stared the more she felt something was calling to her from somewhere in the sky.

Where does it lead?

The white light was getting brighter and brighter, evoking a feeling of warmth. It even seemed to be moving toward her. And she couldn't understand what was happening. It was all too much. Wished she could just wish it away. Wished she'd never seen it.

With even greater effort, she closed her eyes, shutting out the penetrating light. It made her antsy. She refused to open her eyes again until the light was gone. From her position on the ground, she tried to move her head away from it, but that was completely hopeless. She tried to move her legs. Nothing. She felt as if her legs were secured to the ground with restraints. She only relaxed when a deluge of tears fell down her face. But suddenly, as abruptly as the nightmare had started, it was over.

Chapter 42

WHEN Gail woke it was to the faint sunlight filtering through the curtains of the living room window and the sound of birdsong outside. Her eyes fluttered open, and she tried to remember the dream. The details were fuzzy. Only fragments of her dream lingered. Something about being trapped on the ground. Nothing more, but it was enough to make her uneasy.

With certainty, she felt this was no random dream. She thought it might have something to do with the ghost she had seen last night. That she was being haunted. And that she had the dream because of the entity's influence over her mind.

Gail took several minutes to get her bearings, during which time she weighed in her options. It all boiled down to one thing. Should she go or should she stay?

A little sigh escaped her lips at the question. *If she left the cabin, how would she finish her book?* a voice inside her asked.

The cabin was haunted by the ghost of a dead girl. But when it came right down to it, the ghost hadn't done anything wrong. Nothing bad had happened to her, which was good. It was a totally harmless ghost. Or so she hoped.

Still, she had to devise a plan. She closed her eyes, trying to calm her mind. It was times like this she wanted to go birdwatching, to think this through.

Her eyes flew open. Looking pleased with herself, she smiled as she wiggled into a more comfortable position on the couch. Perhaps she'd done enough thinking about it.

Her mind was made up. She was going to tough it out to get a necessary job done. And when Gail decided on something, that was what she did. She'd been that way since she was twelve years old. Plus, as soon as the manuscript was complete, she was getting out of there. Which shouldn't be long now. She was sure tomorrow would be her last day of working on the manuscript.

Clearly still shaken from yesterday's events, she waited sixty seconds, and counted sixty more.

A little reluctantly she rose from the couch. She was still dressed in yesterday's clothes, the same tan pants and the same pink cardigan over the same white blouse dotted with pink and red flowers. But she didn't care. For now, she was more concerned with getting through the day without any kind of ghostly interruption.

On her way to the typewriter, a cold draft of air swept into the room and induced an eerie feeling that someone was standing behind her. As she wheeled around, she was afraid to breathe, or even blink.

No one there! She kept looking around the room to see if the ghost had come back. Now she was acting paranoid. After yesterday's scare, it was to be expected. But she came to her senses. She had to take into consideration the cabin was naturally cool more than usual because of the autumn weather.

Gail resumed her seat behind the typewriter. She fed a piece of clean typewriter paper into the carriage and stared at it, as writers do. Her mind blanked. She placed her hands on the keys and waited. Her eyes became intense. She fidgeted in her seat for a moment, then began typing. Every thought flowed directly from her brain onto the paper.

For the next hour or so, a dark foreboding descended on her thoughts that insisted on straying. She was fearful that the ghost might come into the living room, as if half expecting it to pop up behind her. It was difficult to concentrate on her typing because she couldn't stop stealing glances around the room.

To her relief she hadn't sensed anything. So far, nothing was amiss — no signs of the ghost. But she was still on edge. She couldn't predict if this supernatural being was going to appear at any moment.

After a short pause, she fed paper into her typewriter, and with total concentration began to pound the keys. The hours flew by as she typed rapidly. It was during that time that her paranoia subsided. She began to convince herself that the ghost that had appeared to her in the living room had been part of her strange nightmare. She became even more convinced that she was simply stressed out. Blessed with a vivid imagination, she was a writer after all, her mind was in revolt against the pressure to finish the novel. But even as she told herself that there wasn't any other plausible explanation, there was a minuscule part of her that had to confess that a few times she had felt a presence in the cabin.

That night, she was still tapping away on the typewriter until the sudden rain, yanked her out of her thoughts. She stopped typing altogether, in the middle of a chapter. It wasn't like her. Usually, she didn't stop typing until each chapter was completed.

Leaning back in her chair, she stared into space for ten minutes. Her body shook and shuddered as she listened to the rain pounding the windows and drumming on the roof of the cabin. For reasons she could not explain, the torrent of rain was affecting her mood. It was already after ten o'clock and she wanted to call it a day.

With an exasperated huff, she stared at the page in the typewriter in front of her. It would have to wait until morning. She came up out of the chair as though she'd received an electric shock. It was something she couldn't control. The tat tat tat of heavy rain lashing the windows kept her moody.

Exiting the living room, she disappeared around the corner into the hallway that led to the bedrooms. First thing tomorrow, she'd finish the novel. And with that thought, she went down the hallway in a much better frame of mind than the one she had been in that morning.

Chapter 43

TODAY was Halloween. The weather was cool — no rain, a mild breeze blowing down Monroe Street of Stroudsburg. Most of the houses in the city were decked out for the season. Ghosts made of white bedsheets hung from porches, witches with blinking red lights for eyes stood on the steps, smiling jack-o'-lanterns peered from the windows, and lines of twinkling, black-and-orange lights dangled from the trees.

Inside the Monroe County Courthouse, for the sheriff, it was just another Monday morning at work. He greeted the dispatcher and stopped off in the break room, where he poured himself a mug of coffee. He smiled mischievously as he pulled his hand out of the orange pumpkin bucket filled with candy that sat next to the coffee maker. The Milky Way candy bar would be the perfect treat to go with freshly brewed coffee.

When he stepped out of the break room, he almost bumped into Deputy Missy Sparks.

"Careful, Sparks, the sheriff has a lousy temper and carries a gun. He has been known to lock people up when they spill his drink. And he'll throw away the key, so you have to stay there forever," Chief Deputy Livengood said, who'd been standing in the hallway.

Her eyes wide, Sparks shot a glance at him, then said, "Very funny, Livengood."

They shared a laugh, not something Sparks was sure she should have done, knowing how sensitive Kirkman could be at times. Whereas the chief deputy often entertained them with jokes and funny stories from his years on the job.

"It is so nice to see you both in good spirits. I'll see you, Livengood, for the morning briefing in five minutes," said the sheriff, who then went to his office.

Sometime later that morning, the sheriff's office was quiet. Sheriff Kirkman was catching up on paperwork when he remembered the phone call, he had received from Gillian Wincoff last Friday. What stuck in his mind was that she had told him that Detective Silverwood rarely answered her calls. She left him dozens of phone messages, but he didn't return a single one. She thought he had been sullen and obnoxious the two times she had spoken to him. Knowing Silverwood, the way he did, he didn't contradict her.

Now he was slightly slumped in his chair with a distant look on his face. Every time he imagined what Gillian Wincoff must be going through, it saddened him. Of all the things he'd faced in his tenure as sheriff, nothing was worse for him than dealing with the grieving parent of a missing child.

In all actuality, he was haunted by the possibility of this case remaining unsolved long after his retirement. And just thinking along those lines spooked him out.

Even though his rational brain told him otherwise, this seemed like the right time for him to ring Detective Silverwood. Maybe there was something he could find out that would appease Mrs. Wincoff from her sorrow. There just had to be something. It might have been premature of him to think that, but he wanted to be optimistic, if only temporarily.

He shoved aside his paperwork, picked up the phone and dialed listening to Philip Silverwood's voice after the second ring.

"It's Kirkman. Last Friday afternoon Gillian Wincoff telephoned me wanting to know something about her daughter's case, how we were progressing, and what, if anything, was going on. I didn't have anything new to tell her. I want to know if you have any news on the case?"

The detective said nothing for a couple of moments, then approximated a sniff. "Well, I only have a few minutes to talk. Right now, there are more pressing matters to be dealt with on my desk. Actually, this is not a good time — can I call you back later?"

Sheriff Kirkman was beside himself with frustration. Silverwood didn't sound pleased to hear his voice and was making up excuses not to talk to him as he went along.

"For Christ's sake! How long can it possibly take to check the notes on the case file?" Kirkman asked in an insistent tone.

The sheriff had to be persistent. But was he wasting his time? In some small part of his mind, he wondered, with the election taking place in less than two weeks, whether the detective was dissing him.

"All right, just hold on," Silverwood said in a bothered tone.

Kirkman breathed in deeply, and bit back the growl of frustration at being left on hold. He sat hunched in his chair, elbows-on-the-desk, the telephone receiver in his hand. It just irked him that Silverwood had been assigned to lead the Abigail Wincoff case, organizing it, looking for clues and so forth.

He had waited three minutes listening to dead air and then Silverwood was back on the line. The detective told him there had been no sightings of Abigail Wincoff and nothing new to report. There had been no movement on the case in days. No body. Nothing. Then he ended the call before Kirkman could say any more.

Listening to the detective's reactions made the obvious even more obvious. Not only was Kirkman upset that the Abigail Wincoff case had reached a standstill, but already he didn't like the way Detective Silverwood was handling it. Because the detective seemed to have hit a dead end, the sheriff worried the case was going cold fast unless a new lead turned up.

He returned to his paperwork with the goal of sorting through it and filing it away. He often found himself dealing with the constant barrage of paperwork which was never really finished. After that, he planned to spend the rest of his shift on the roads, keeping the streets safe from drunk drivers celebrating Halloween.

Chapter 44

AFTER PARKING her Toyota in the lot of her employer, Clean As A Whistle, Millie Dozier headed toward the office. It was payday Friday, and she was going to get her hair done this afternoon. Once a month, she treated herself to a visit to a salon, where she enjoyed being pampered and fussed over as her hair was shampooed. She fully indulged in the luxury of her hairdresser's agile fingers massaging her scalp.

Her other indulgence when she got paid was spoiling her two Abyssinian cats with treats. Her beloved cats were her companions, and she was devoted to them.

Stepping through the door, she saw that the receptionist and secretary, a sleek, well-preserved Latina in her mid-fifties, was talking on the phone. She walked toward the desk with a smile on her face. In the midst of her conversation, she handed Millie an envelope.

"Thank you, Celia," she whispered quickly.

As she turned around, Celia put her hand over the phone. "Hold on a moment. I have you on the schedule for tomorrow. Somewhere else. Wait, and I will give you the details."

Millie turned back around, nodded politely, and sat down in a chair facing the desk. A couple of minutes afterward, Celia finished her call.

"Earlier this morning I spoke with the owner of the cabin on Wagon Trail Road. Chief Deputy Livengood of the Monroe County Police Department had called to inform him that the cabin was no longer considered a crime scene. Now that the police have released the cabin back to the owner, he has requested our services. I want you to go over there tomorrow morning," she said quickly, almost running out of breath.

"What about the cabin in Dingmans Ferry?" Millie asked.

"Marisa has already been scheduled to take your place," said Celia.

"I will be happy to oblige," Millie said, sounding slightly reluctant.

"I'm rather busy. Anything else?"

"No. Have a pleasant day," Millie said, and got up from the chair to leave.

When Millie got into her car and drove away, she was aware that the grim sense of premonition was with her. She stared straight ahead, eyes on the road as she thought back to that day, she'd reported a break-in at the cabin on Wagon

Trail Road. She remembered the horrid, whispery voice in the cabin and how she felt an otherworldly presence.

Someone honked at her. Green light. She'd sat there for almost a minute, head in the clouds. Bad omen. She drove through the intersection. Another honk! She honked back. Then she continued driving for another couple of blocks, keeping her eyes peeled as she drove a little faster than before.

Her mind wandered off again. This time she was reminiscing about her younger years. The day after her husband proposed to her, she went to her favorite spot near the bayou. For the longest time, she sat against a worn-down, bleached white cypress tree, dreaming about her wedding day. She stared moodily at the sun darting its rays through the mist, while the pea-green bayou water bobbed on the surface. Oh, how she missed the trips to the bayou. But missed her late husband the most.

After stopping at the bank long enough to deposit her paycheck, she drove eagerly to the hair salon.

The bell on the door chimed as she pushed her way through. The small but stylish black-and-white-tiled hair salon was mostly empty. Her nose pricked up from the hint of jojoba shampoo and hair spray in the air. In the middle of a yawn, she sat down in the reception area to wait.

Millie was snapped out of her doze by the sound of her name being called out. She tensed at the sound of the voice. Her handbag slipped to the floor.

Picking up her bag from the floor, she noticed the bulletin board near the register. It was papered with homemade flyers advertising babysitters, cars for sale and yard sales. One of them caught her eye. It was printed in a bold typeface with a photo, the Missing Child flyer of Abigail Wincoff.

Without realizing it, she drifted over to look at it. As she ran her eyes down it, she thought it was an odd coincidence, remembering how she had stared at it, fascinated. All the same, she had no idea where she'd put the one the TV reporter had given her. It was still affecting her. She stared numbly into the face of the young Abigail Wincoff, believing she'd seen her before. But where? And how?

The sound of her name being called again kept her from falling into a trance. At her workstation the hairdresser, a dainty young Chinese woman in floral blouse and tight navy-blue trousers, shifted her feet impatiently, waiting for Millie with a disgruntled look on her face.

With a disappointed sigh, Millie slowly turned away from the Missing Child flyer. It depressed her so.

Seemingly preoccupied, Millie started walking toward the hairdresser, her crossed eyes shifted catching sight of the black hair in the hairdresser's chair. As soon as she was seated in the swivel styling chair, she stared at herself in the mirror.

Right off the bat, the hairdresser looked at her in a puzzled way. And as she did, Millie looked at her, confusion clouding her eyes.

"Everything okay, Millie? I just asked you how you were doing," the hairdresser told her.

"Oh, pardon me, Sue Ling. My mind was somewhere else. I'm doing fine, actually. Thank you for asking," she responded graciously.

Millie decided she wasn't going to dwell on this missing girl. Knowing she had to refocus her thoughts, she simply smiled at the hairdresser.

Chapter 45

AS Millie Dozier turned her car onto Wagon Trail Road, her crossed eyes narrowed, apprehension shimmering through her gaze. And when she got closer to the chestnut log cabin, something inside her twinged. Despite her feelings, she parked her car near a little grove of trees anxious to get to work.

Millie hopped out of the car, her crossed eyes darting around as she walked toward the cabin. She didn't sense anything unusual until she approached the front door. Her ears perked up to the clack of typewriter keys. Her panic spiked. Who would be in the cabin? The typing came again, louder, and more intense as she moved closer.

She put her ear against the door, straining to hear. There was a new sound from inside the cabin — a guttural noise that sounded like a growl.

Heart hammering, she spun away from the door, suddenly overcome with a desire to get back in her car and leave but stopped herself. After a breath or two, she turned back around, and put her ear to the door again.

Complete silence.

Dear God, was she hearing things? Or was she just paranoid?

She lifted her head. Deciding to play it safe, she opened the door just a crack, hearing nothing but the sound of her heart beating. When she poked her head inside, she clearly saw a typewriter on a veneer side table in the corner of the living room. But nobody was there. Her crossed eyes twinged into a suspicious expression that left no room for doubt that she was going to be cautious in doing her job.

A mildew smell accompanied her entry into the cabin. It was empty, cool, and dusty. Her first task was to change the linens on the beds. Not much later, she was cleaning and disinfecting the bathroom. Over a half an hour had gone by, and all was quiet.

A shadow crept past the doorway of the bathroom, but she didn't catch it. Then she closed the mirrored medicine cabinet door and failed to see the reflection of Abby's ghost in the mirror. Abby was directly behind her now, in the doorway with her doll clasped tightly to her chest. But Millie's back was turned to her, and she was too engrossed in her work to notice. Just seconds before she left the bathroom, Abby's ghost had vanished.

Millie picked up a feather duster, came into the living room and went to work. On impulse, she started whistling a Cajun tune about life on the bayou, rump shaking her way around the room. With the amount of energy she'd burned, she was already looking forward to having lunch later in the day. And she was craving a bowl of perfectly spiced crawfish gumbo and a loaf of hot buttered French bread. The thought pleased her, and she smiled as she put down her feather duster on the side table by the couch.

The tune seemed to stir something in Abby's spirit, who was floating around the attic. Surely enough, she started humming the "Little Bunny Foo Foo" tune loud enough for Millie to hear through the ventilation ducts.

Just as Millie drew back the curtains from the window, she stopped whistling and winced against the sunlight that cut across her face. Her expression changed into one of disbelief. This was no hallucination. Her response was restrained at first, but within moments she crossed over to stand under a heating and cooling vent in the ceiling.

It was nothing she could easily identify, but she had heard it before with the same intonation of a child. She had heard the eerie melody that day in August she called the police to report the break-in. She stood there like a feral cat ready to run for cover if anyone made the slightest move toward her.

Just like that, the humming stopped. The room was perfectly quiet now. And after a short wait, Millie felt compelled to return to her work despite a growing fear that something was wrong about the place, whether it was ghosts — or not — which she could only assume.

In her agitated state dusting the windows had escaped her mind. She grabbed the feather duster and went to work on the table with the typewriter on it. It was then that Abby beelined for her, which sent a cold burst of air all around her. Rattled, Millie felt a cold chill skitter up her spine, reverberating along her very receptive nerves, and she froze in her tracks.

"Stay away," Abby shrilled in terror.

The sound carried loudly in the quiet and echoed through the cabin. Millie convinced herself that whatever produced the sound wasn't of this earth. She stiffened, willing herself not to react to what she'd heard, and for half a minute she actually managed it.

Millie's crossed eyes narrowed to slits and she clenched her hands together. An unseen force was preventing her from taking another step. Abby was moving around the table where the typewriter was, blocking her from it, rage contorting her ghostly face. Though she had no intention of harming Millie, she was angry enough to scare her.

She needed to refocus her mind. With all the strength Millie could muster, she squared her shoulders and willed herself to break free of this spell, turning away from the table and typewriter. She vowed she wouldn't give this entity the satisfaction of knowing it startled her in any way.

Walking with conviction from the living room, she went to get out the vacuum cleaner. Hurriedly, she vacuumed the rugs, looking around every so often for any trace of movement. There was none. But the whole time she had the distinct impression that she was being watched in the living room. Even though she could see that the room was empty, she couldn't shake the uneasy feeling that someone was there, watching her.

Beyond any shadow of a doubt, Millie's instincts were right. The sound of the vacuum cleaner roared with full force and drowned out the barely audible whispering coming from the other side of the living room. The ghost of Abby was there. Watching.

When Millie finished, she gathered her things and headed for the front door. As she walked down the hallway with a sense of unease, she couldn't wait to get out of there.

After starting the car, she drove away from the cabin and couldn't help but look in her rearview mirror. A chill worked its way through her body, the same cold feeling she'd experienced in the living room of the cabin.

As she focused on the road ahead, she decided to keep this to herself. She worried that people might think she was losing it, even if she knew she wasn't. In the future, if her employer assigned her to work there again, she planned to fake illness so they would send somebody else to take her place.

Still, she couldn't fathom what had happened in the cabin. Immersed in her thoughts, she barely noticed the turn-off coming up. When she slowed down to make the turn onto another street, she unconsciously began to hum the "Little Bunny Foo Foo" tune.

The spell didn't last too long. Almost immediately afterwards, she shook out of it in time to realize.

To her dismay she said, "By God."

She crossed herself quickly before flooring her gas pedal. Tires screeching, she sped the car off Wagon Trail Road and onto the next road. Head up, heart racing, hands clutched tightly to the steering wheel, she kept the car under control.

On days like this, she wanted to retire early and carry out her plan to return to that sleepy Louisiana bayou town of Plaquemine, where she would share a house with her two cats. And on warm, sunny days she would sit in her rocking chair looking out over the bayou.

Chapter 46

THE RAIN had come again, just after midnight. While Gail had slept, a ceiling of gray clouds hung over the cabin, unleashing shower after shower of rain. At five a.m. the rain had stopped and the storm clouds in the sky had broken, leaving behind a gray mist around the cabin.

Just as the sun was starting to rise above the Pocono Mountains, Abigail Wincoff's ghostly face peered into the living room window, the only one with the curtains drawn. Her gaze fell upon Gail who was sleeping on the couch. All too clearly, she could see that Gail lay curled on her side, facing the room, one hand curled over her head.

Another minute or two, and then the ghost of Abby had vanished.

A goldfinch scolded furiously perched on the branch of a pine tree near the cabin. The sun's rays penetrated the tree canopy and shone through the high, basement window, which was half above the ground, half submerged. The low-ceilinged basement had beige walls and a wooden floor. The temperature of the room was ten degrees cooler than the rest of the cabin.

A low moaning sound came from the center of the room. In the semidarkness, Abigail Wincoff appeared from thin air, simply materializing from within the center of an anomaly. A convergence of spirit and swirling matter fused into an almost solid form, and then broke apart. It reshaped itself, forming quickly into the image of a brown-haired little girl, wearing a white dress.

Rattling about, her spirit maneuvered to the corner of the room facing the curtainless, narrow window. Her black eyes were staring ahead at nothing, while her doll swung from her hand. She hovered above the spot on the floorboard where her body was completely buried in the earth three feet below. Although, it was difficult to tell, because there was no smell of rotting flesh.

She clutched her doll to her chest and rocked it gently. Her body swaying back and forth, she slowly spun around in the empty room.

"Help me," she screamed.

No one could hear her. No one knew she was there. She was many miles away from anyone who knew her when she was alive. Every time she screamed, she evoked a strong feeling of loneliness and despair. There so much turmoil within her.

It did no good, but she screamed again. "Help me."

With a spine-chilling moan, Abby's ghostly figure rose a few feet into the air. The room began to shimmer as her form slowly dematerialized.

Right around the time Abby's spirit vanished, Gail woke to the odors of mid-autumn in the living room. With renewed energy and sense of purpose, she uncurled her body with a lazy stretch and got up from the couch. She wanted to get back to her novel. She would write a death scene that would leap off the page, bring tears to the eyes of her readers, and fill her existence with everything that was missing.

She moved to the typewriter, all the while wondering if she had somehow lost track of the days. It seemed to her as though all the days were rolled into one long day that was still nowhere near ending. There was a lot she didn't remember, but she had been so involved in her writing that this had only just occurred to her.

It was stress, that was all it was, she told herself as she sank into her chair. A look of intense concentration came over her face, and she went back to her typing, knowing these would be the last pages for her book.

The attic stairs were pulled down, a foul, cool breeze wafting from inside. The ghost of Abby was lurking around the room. The doll hung loosely from her hand. She moved toward the small, circular window, whispering, followed by a string of monotonous murmuring.

Something was stirring within her. As she stared morosely out the window, staring at nothing in particular, somehow her black eyes appeared to be fixated on a random point in the woods.

It was mid-afternoon when Gail had typed and set the last page, face down on top of the others in a neat stack on the table beside the typewriter. Just like she had planned, she had finished her psychological thriller novel, *Murder in the Poconos*.

She sighed, relaxed her shoulders, and slumped against the back of the chair. *This was the best thing she had ever done*, Gail thought, feeling a sense of peace sweep over her. She was hungry to share the news with someone, anyone — but nobody came to mind.

Brilliant sunlight poured across the living room. She scanned the room, pleased to see the curtains were drawn on one of the windows. She got up and wandered over to take a look outside.

After a long interval of staring blankly out the window, all she could think to do was to go birdwatching. This would be her last chance now that she would be leaving here. The weather was perfect for it. It was a bright, sunny afternoon with nothing but a blue sky. All indications of the storm that had blanketed the area with heavy rain in the predawn hours were gone.

For the next fifteen minutes, she made her way through the cabin, searching every room with the methodical intensity of a madwoman. She couldn't find her binoculars. *Where could they be?* she thought as she entered the living room.

Gail finally gave up searching for the binoculars. Birdwatching was off the table now. She was ready to leave the cabin. With that decision made, she tore out of the living room and headed down the hallway.

Chapter 47

AN undetermined amount of time later, Gail came back into the living room. She tuned in to the noise coming through an air vent in the ceiling. It sounded like it was coming from the attic. It was the same low, murmuring sound over and over again, terrible little intervals of silence in-between.

She was just debating whether she should go and check it out when the noise stopped momentarily. Then, it resumed again, steady, and insistent. That was when it occurred to her that perhaps it might be that ghost. Maybe there really was a ghost haunting the cabin. She had to consider the possibility all over again.

Quietly, she made her way down the hallway. She'd no desire to stay here any longer, but neither could she ignore this opportunity to discover what was causing the noise. Whether there really was a ghost or not was important. This way, she would know whether she had dreamt it or not.

Could she be dreaming now?

The heavy old, creaking attic stairs took a bit of effort to pull down. She looked up the stairs, listening with her ears pricked. At first there was nothing. Then she heard a faint whimpering sound.

Gail moved back slowly, careful not to make any noise. Her eyelids were fluttering. She wasn't sure of what to do next. Should she climb the stairs?

"I slid to the ground and the man in the shadows stepped forward. He kept hitting me, whipping me until I bled," came a ghostly voice from nowhere and everywhere.

Fear squeezed her chest. It was the same ghostly voice she'd heard before, the tormented voice of the ghost of the little girl that she'd seen in the living room.

She eyed the stairs. It was as if an uncontrollable force was pushing her forward. She began to wonder if she had been led here on purpose.

With some reluctance, she slowly walked up the stairs, feeling like she didn't have a choice anymore. She braced herself for whatever was waiting for her.

To her surprise, there was no one there at all. She heard no voices, either. But for a chilling moment, she wondered whether she was under monumental stress. On a positive note, she believed there had been no ghost in the cabin, which dissolved away the source of tension from her face.

Her eyes dropped down and lingered momentarily on the doll on the floor. She shrugged and moved her eyes to the circular window in the corner near a wooden table with a television on the top, and then to a photograph of a little girl on the floor. A storm of sensation swept through her. It felt known, which was as impossible as it was ridiculous.

What was it about the photograph that made it feel familiar to her?

Genuine curiosity got the better of her. She walked over, bent to look at it, and picked up the photo for a closer look. For quite a long time, she just stood there, staring at it in her hand. Because somehow, buried deep in her memory, she recognized it as a picture of her twelve-year-old self on a bicycle taken by her Grandmother Louise in Watchung, New Jersey.

"It can't be. No. It can't," she kept saying to herself, over and over.

A shudder went through her. She felt dizzy, numbly holding the photograph of her younger self, which suddenly weighed a ton. She took a step back and it slithered out of her hand and onto the floor.

The trill of a little girl's giggling filled the air just before a voice came booming into the room. "I'm so afraid. Can you help me?"

Gail turned in the direction of the voice to find the ghost of Abigail Wincoff floating in front of her, staring into her eyes with a mesmerizing intensity. Looking at Abby was like looking into a mirror. Gail saw herself, fifteen years younger. The eyes were small, the skin soft, and the hair sandy brown like her father, Lance's. And yet, she had her mother, Gillian's features.

Why hadn't she noticed it before?

There was a ghost in the cabin, after all, and it was real. Gail was the one that wasn't real, but a figment of an imagination desperate for resolution. The fact was that Abby and herself were one and the same. Abby had invented her for a purpose and because she was so lonely. It was as if Gail had been an imaginary friend that she had played with, but only for a while. Now that her writing task was completed, she was no longer needed.

It was very clever of Abby. Like a dream, but real, Gail was an astral projection all along. Abby's mind was able to be in two places at once. In spirit form, she reappeared somewhere else as someone else. In this case, she was Gail, a ghostwriter to tell her story. And she had played her part to the hilt. And Abby could snap back to herself at any time. It took some practice, not without a few glitches and lapses of time along the way, but she soon mastered it.

Gail remembered. Oh, did she remember. The child inside herself wanted to grow up to be her. She wanted to exist, but she knew it was not possible. She wanted to cry, but there were no tears left. There was nothing but an empty feeling.

And then it flashed into her mind, a traumatic memory came flooding back to her. Her head shook in exasperation, trying to dispel the horrible memory, but no luck. Her mind filled with images she couldn't suppress any longer. The room darkened, and darkened some more, and suddenly her legs wobbled out from beneath her. She slid to the floor, landing flatly on her bottom.

As she thought back to that horrible day in August, the projection that had been Gail would soon be no more.

Chapter 48

Tuesday, August 23, 2016

BY THE SOUND of twigs breaking, someone was moving through the woods. At the time, Abigail Wincoff didn't think anything of it because the sounds of the birds and insects was what stood out to her. Watching her from the corner of his eye, serial killer Joey Marks, aka Ryan Messer followed her, hidden in the soft shadows of the pine trees. She was too young and naïve and couldn't understand that someone was watching her, following her, planning to do something awful to her.

Abby was south of the cabin, less than a quarter of a mile from Meadow Lake, and near Wagon Trail Road. But she didn't know where she was. Somewhere along the way, she'd gotten lost. Thoughts of finding her way back consumed her mind.

And that was the beginning of the end.

A branch snapped in the woods she had been facing — and it made her nervous. Someone — something — was there with her. Twigs crackled underfoot. Whatever was making those sounds, was making its way toward her, no longer bothering to be quiet.

Before the sounds, she had been thinking about her parents. Now, all she could think about were the sounds.

Just for the heck of it, Abby looked over her shoulder. At first glance there seemed to be no one present. The woods became deathly quiet. As she turned her head away, a blur of movement beside a tree caught her eye. Nervously, she glanced again over her shoulder. Peering hard, she made out a shadow. Fear gripped her. She blinked to clear her vision. The shadow blended with other shadows. She didn't need to raise her binoculars. Had she just imagined that someone was there?

She didn't see him coming.

A savage blow slammed her forward. The air exploded from her lungs, and she doubled over in pain, the sudden shock depriving her of most of her senses. Before she could look to see who'd hit her, a fist sunk into her stomach. As she fell onto her knees, the binoculars fell to the ground. The strap of the binoculars had torn. She drifted a moment in that position.

Suddenly she was kicked in the back, and she keeled over. A small flock of birds took flight from a nearby tree, frightened, while the other sounds of nature faded. All she could see were his boots. He trapped her, standing over her, legs astride.

With a groan, she rolled onto her side to face him. She gazed up into his eyes, her breathing coming in sobs. He gave her a gentle smile, pinning her with a sideways glance that seemed to look right through to her soul. He looked as innocent as a lamb.

He wasn't.

His eyebrows peaked, his head tilted, and his mouth twisted into a sadistic grin. With it she saw temper burn across his face.

Through a haze of shock and pain, Abby rolled over onto her stomach and started to get up. When she was halfway up on her knees, he kicked her in the back, in the kidney, and she pitched over on her face.

Abigail Wincoff begged for her life. "Stop! Please stop! Help me! I'm begging you."

Her agonized face pleaded for mercy, but there was none coming. In fact, the more she pleaded, the more this madman wanted to stomp her into the dirt.

He memorized her expression, the panic in her eyes and let the sound of her grunts forge a permanent imprint in his mind. Then he bent over and ran a hand through her hair.

"Shh," he whispered, and the sound sliced through the air like the blade of a long-handled billhook.

Again, squaring her shoulders, she tried to get onto her hands and knees to stand up and found it was impossible. Eyes blazing, he shot her a look of seething dislike. As if her trying to get up had sparked off some terrible rage that had been deep inside him for so long. He kicked the small of her back, kicked a knee, and kicked her in the head over and over again. Wielding that power of inflicting pain had hit his system like an addictive drug.

Everything was happening too fast for Abby to really process. Waves of faintness washed over her. Her head was throbbing in pain. She lay breathing harshly and rapidly, unable to move from the pain. She tried to cry out to him again, to plead for her life and beg him to stop, but could only let out a whimper, barely a sound at all.

When he was done, he sighed just slightly and stepped back a few paces. He blinked once, looking skywards, and then he blinked again and looked down at his hands. They were clenched into tight fists from building tension. His nails were digging into his palms, but not enough to break the skin. Slowly, he forced his fists to open, and the tension eased.

Blood dribbled down the side of her cheek and onto the neck of her white dress. Abby was gagging.

"Help me," she gurgled in an agonizing tone.

It did her no good. However hard she tried, her words weren't loud enough for anyone but Joey Marks to hear, even though nobody was around to overhear her. She wasn't going to get any help. She was alone. And being alone was the most frightening thing to her.

He planted himself in front of her, watching her hand twitch. She felt black unconsciousness swirling around her, devouring her life. She could feel the wet gush of blood spurting from her nose even though a whirlpool of nausea churned her insides.

Now, Abby was barely conscious, her eyes half-lidded. From her lips came a long-drawn-out moan, totally exhausted, and resigned to her fate. Her body twitched three times, and then her muscles locked in a final spasm. Abigail Wincoff was dead.

At least her body was.

After she went limp, he waited several minutes to be sure. He cast a careful glance around him and was relieved there was no one around. He walked around her, raised his eyebrows as his eyes slowly scanned her body, trailing from her head and down to her back.

A lot of time had passed since the spasm that her skin had turned pale and waxy. There was a delicious delight in knowing she was dead. Energized by that knowledge made him close his eyes in ecstasy.

Joey Marks had beaten Abigail Wincoff to death, with punches and kicks for no good reason at all. She might have been struck forty times or more. Head trauma — that was what killed her — but she would have died anyway from her other injuries.

After opening his eyes, he grinned wryly, staring at her lifeless body. He didn't know her name and didn't bother to ask. Neither did he care. All that mattered to him was that he was pleased with the killing.

The muscle along his jaw began to twitch as images formed in his mind. Her mother would want to know where she was. Her worried mother, crying. Her worried father, searching the woods.

Marks breathed in deep, struggling to keep himself calm, but second by second his nerves were winding up like a clockwork engine. He gritted his teeth, thinking too much time had already passed. He desperately wanted to get away from the area, but he had to bury Abby's body. So, he couldn't leave.

Chapter 49

JOEY MARKS pulled a pair of latex gloves from the front pocket of his black jeans and put them on over the stickiness of Abby's blood on his hands. After throwing a quick glance over his shoulder to make sure he was unobserved, he rummaged around in his black sling bag he'd put on the ground. He withdrew a folded-up, canvas builder's bag. And a roll of black duct tape. He moved closer to her, being as quiet as possible as he bound her arms and legs with duct tape. It took some doing, but he managed to cram her inside the bag in a reasonable amount of time.

He pulled up a patch of bloodstained grass and shoved it into the bag. When and if minuscule traces of her blood were found, he could only hope he'd be long gone by that time. For that reason, he needed to buy some time to flee the vicinity. So, he thought himself very clever to leave the binoculars where they lie. And in doing so indicated she'd been there. *They'd think she was lost somewhere within, that she had strayed*, he thought. They would concentrate all their efforts on finding the missing girl, wandering aimlessly in the woods.

And they wouldn't find her.

A worried expression on his face, he was mumbling softly to himself as he swung the bag with her in it over his shoulder. He couldn't help it. As he carried her off in the direction of Wagon Trail Road, he thought about stopping. He became worried in turn and mumbled to himself some more. But not loud enough to be heard from a distance, and in that regard, could only be heard by someone in close proximity to him.

As he approached the cabin, the only sounds were the flutter of birds in the branches, the buzzing insects, and his boots brushing through the grass and crushing twigs underfoot. Moving carefully, he gently set the bag on the ground at the side of the cabin where the basement was. Poking around until he found the shovel he had hidden under the foundation; he knew what he had to do next.

Over the next thirty minutes, like a man obsessed, he dug a shallow hole about four feet long and three feet wide beneath the basement floor, at times stopping to rest. Beneath his gloves, tiny blisters were forming across the palms, for he had been moving too fast. But he had too.

More troublesome was that his digging had stirred up a swarm of mosquitoes, which flew toward him. Not to mention the mildew-like odor coming from underneath the basement's floor. Deep in concentration, he couldn't stop now. Instinct told him time was running thin.

With an ill-stifled groan, he stopped digging. He slumped against the mound of dirt that stood to one side, swiping mosquitoes out if his face.

Less than two minutes later, he looked down into the hole. It was the perfect place to hide a body. Forcefully he shoved the bag into the hole. He took up the shovel again and filled it in, before pushing the shovel into the dirt, burying it with the body. With an odd feeling of finality, he patted the dirt down with his gloved hands until no one could tell the ground had been disturbed.

The burial was complete.

At this time, he could only think about how he needed to wipe the blood off his hands and forearms. He decided to break into the cabin and wash up in the kitchen sink.

As if angered by his presence, the crows arrived to flap above the cabin and complained noisily from nearby trees. The cawing, flapping crows that scattered in all directions and the hum of the mosquitoes that seemed to grow louder by tiny degrees with each passing minute was too much for him.

The bones in his back cracked as he straightened and began a walk around the cabin. The window near the front door was large enough for him to fit. He kicked, over and over, until the glass smashed. His mind racing, he worried about the noise, but he was too far along to stop now. Without further ado, he reached inside, unlocked the window, and slid it open. He climbed through, his feet crunching the broken glass on the wood floor. Lastly, he pulled the window shut, locked it, keeping the curtains closed. Maybe no one would notice the broken pane from outside.

Standing at the kitchen sink, he turned on the cold water, then peeled off his gloves and stuffed them into his back jeans pocket. He leaned over and put his face in the stream and drank several mouthfuls, before washing his hands.

His mind drifted as he let the water run over his hands. The next moment he thought about how most of the kids at his school either ignored him or taunted him. Years of insidious bullying had led to anger issues and fights in school. And no one wanted to be his friend. His mouth tightened, remembering the climate in which he grew up.

The kids shouted in his mind. "Blockhead Joey."

In ninth grade he'd learned an important lesson. There were plenty of students like him, who were willing to use violence as he was. Rudy Pena was his name. A Mexican American punk, in his eyes. Picked him out for a fight. Rudy had gone into a fighting stance, bare-handed, the look in his eyes wild. Anger swelled in Joey's chest. He lunged at him, placed his hands around his throat, choking Rudy till he almost passed out. Whatever had been going on in that warped head of his, Rudy obviously hadn't anticipated this kind of kink in his plans.

"If you mess with me again, I'll kill you," a teenage Joey warned.

Rudy believed him. It was a good thing he did, too.

Run now, a little voice whispered in his head.

Marks reached over and turned off the faucet. He shook the excess water off his hands before wiping them on the back of his jeans. Then he pulled a handkerchief from his shirt pocket and wiped the faucet handle, rubbing off fingerprints.

As he strolled through the living room, his eyes caught sight of a *Natural History* magazine on the side table beside the couch. The issue pictured the Adirondacks on the cover. He walked over, rolled the magazine up and stuffed it into the sling bag hanging over his shoulder.

The front door squeaked open. He stood in the doorway as he wiped the doorknob with his handkerchief. With a devious look, his eyes roamed around to make sure no one was lurking about outside. After a moment's thought, he left, the door slamming shut on its own.

Chapter 50

TO HIS twisted way of thinking, Joey Marks felt justified in his actions in killing Abigail Wincoff, and didn't care a thing about her personally. But there could be no legitimate reason for what he'd done to her, no reason that made any sort of sense, no justification. To his victims, he was living proof that evil was real and had a face.

Whistling softly and tunelessly between his teeth, he traveled through the woods with silent steps. He was walking in the direction that led to the clearing surrounded by trees where he had parked his truck earlier in the day.

After a kill, the details were fresh in his mind. His heart would accelerate, adrenaline surging, every cell, every nerve alert. That was what he liked the most, the way it played over and over in his mind. But all too soon those memories faded too quickly, and he would become increasingly anxious, and experience sudden bursts of anger. He had a taste for blood. It was something he couldn't ignore. He knew he would have absolutely no peace of mind if he didn't give in to this incredible desire to kill.

First and foremost was his need to kill and not be caught. Driven by the compulsion to kill, he generally fit the classic stereotype of a white male serial killer. He didn't have any friends, kept to himself. He was physically average and looked younger, appearing to be somewhere between twenty-five and thirty years old.

From a few yards away, Marks heard movement in the woods and spotted what looked like a woman. He dropped down into a crouch, checking left, then right, before he quickly moved behind a tree. For all he knew, she could be a police officer. Though it seemed too early, he had to take into consideration the possibility that the little girl's parents had already called the police to look for her.

For a short span of time, he stood very still, his mind in torment. He could feel faint traces of sweat starting to form on his forehead. Then, very carefully, he peeked around the tree trunk. Considering the distance, he scrutinized her from head to toe. He couldn't make out what she was wearing, just that she didn't have a duty belt on. A wave of relief swept through him accompanied by an exhale. He was certain in his mind that she wasn't a member of the police force. Also, he didn't see or hear anyone else in the woods. It struck him odd that the woman was out here by herself and seemed to be looking around for something.

So, he just waited and watched as she leaned against a tree. Not much longer after that she started walking in the direction of the cabin, where he knew that girl had been staying with her parents.

Could she be that little girl's mother? Yes, probably she was, he thought.

As he watched her leave, he felt jealous. Back when he was younger, his mother never cared to come looking for him.

Standing there he could feel his demons stir. And now it was him that was leaning against the tree trunk, thinking thoughts he'd much rather not think. It wasn't enough that his grandparents had provided him a loving home. He was too damaged by the loss of his mother. A sense of longing welled up inside him as he remembered the times, he had wished she would have visited him. So many times, he found himself wondering … if she hadn't died, would she have tried to visit him?

How she died and all, was something he wasn't proud of, considering her career as a topless dancer at a joint called Classy Lady in Gouldsboro, a city in Monroe County Pennsylvania. In September 1997, she had been strangled to death in her car, allegedly by a serial killer who had been preying on strippers. Even more unusual was that he was attracted to killing in quite the same way the man who killed his mother was.

A few weeks ago, he had read about the murder case of Randee Rae Devereux, her stripper name, on the Internet, only to find out that the case had been solved due to the hard work of the Monroe County Sheriff's Office. Her killer had been caught and was behind bars awaiting trial. And it was their duty to inform the next of kin, him being her son and all, the progress of a police investigation. The old police case files on his mother's murder should have his grandparent's contact information. Although it was unlikely that the police would track him down using that method. His grandparents didn't know where he lived. He hadn't spoken to them in years. He didn't care about them one way or another, certainly not enough to seek them out after years of no contact.

On the downside, every time he thought about his mother anger rotted over him. At the time of her death was when all his troubles at school started. He was twelve years old and forced to grow up too soon. To lessen his torment, in the years that would follow, he had wanted nothing more than to inflict his pain on others.

Still, she was his mother. In her memory, he had vowed to come to Pennsylvania. So here he was in the woods of the Pocono Mountains.

Taking a long look around, he decided he'd wasted enough time and stepped out from behind the tree. His mind was still a jumble of crazy thoughts — about getting away, about the girl he'd killed, about his mother. Nervously, he hurried his steps, eyes downcast, not paying attention to his surroundings. In his haste, he got turned around and lost his way somewhere. It took fifteen more minutes before he finally headed in the right direction. He was out of breath when he finally approached his Silverado pickup truck at a little after noon.

Yes, it was all going to be smooth sailing from here, whistling as he came onto Sellersville Drive. Donning a Baltimore Orioles baseball cap pulled low on his head, he felt exuberant, invincible and a bit smart, too, as he believed he had committed the perfect murder. In the distance, a white Toyota Camry Solara was approaching in the opposite lane, the only other car on the road.

Chapter 51

November 2016

SOMETHING Joey Marks couldn't comprehend was the supernatural aspect of the death of Abigail Wincoff. Would he even care? Most likely not. After all these months, he was settled back in California and comfortable in his job. Abigail Wincoff was nothing but a faded memory. He was already planning a trip somewhere, planning to commit another murder.

The afternoon was ending and there was a brisk wind building. The deep blue sky of late autumn had begun to fade with the sun's slow descent into the west. Leaves in the trees rustled, and everywhere birds were chattering in the trees. In this peaceful setting, the empty, chestnut log cabin on Wagon Trail Road looked anything but haunted.

272 | Ann Greyson

A goldfinch sat on a tree and began to chirp just as the apparition of Abigail Wincoff appeared, barely visible in silhouette against the glare of the last remaining rays of the sun. As she moved toward the cabin, her ghostly image was wobbling against the wind as though she were an extension of the wind itself.

The door opened on its own. The ghost of Abby entered the cabin and stood in the doorway. The wind whipped around from behind, and slammed the door shut behind her. She lingered there a few extra moments, hugging her doll to her chest, murmuring inarticulate sounds.

Seconds after Abigail Wincoff had died, there was a confusion churning inside her. Didn't want to leave the living world. She wanted to live. What was also strange was that she wanted to grow old, wondering what kind of woman she would have become if not for her murder. For a second, she had imagined what it would be like to be older.

The next moment, she had fully accepted that she was dead. But she wouldn't cross over to the next world. So, she was trapped in a state of limbo, a nebulous location somewhere between the living and the dead.

The absence of noise made her feel so horribly alone. She'd wondered if there were other trapped souls like her around. Thus far, she hadn't seen any spirits. From the depths of her soul, she believed there had to be. She could sense it.

Abby was no longer by the door, but there was a low, ghostly whisper drifting through a vent in the living room ceiling. She was there. She would always be there.

The completed manuscript, *Murder in the Poconos*, still stacked beside the typewriter on the table, as though the pile of beautifully typed pages were just waiting for someone to come along and read them. Whoever did read it would discover how Abigail Wincoff had died and where her body had been buried. They didn't have to look far to find her body either. And if her killer was caught, and brought to justice, no other girls would have to suffer her fate.

How long before someone found it? Closure for Abby's family was important. But when would it come? This would help to restore some meaning to her life, the little years she had spent on this Earth. And those years were precious to her.

Abby swore that she would wait for all eternity. She had no other plans for her future. It was important to her to witness the manuscript's discovery. She simply had to.

When she first had the idea to write a book about her life and death, it felt like a good concept for someone alive, but not for someone dead. On that day in August, her killer had just finished burying her body. Her spirit had drifted through the cabin, eventually stopped at the typewriter table in the living room. How badly she wanted to tell everyone what had happened to her, especially her parents. She loved her parents and wished nothing more than to be with them again.

How could she make contact with the living world? She didn't believe it was possible for the dead to communicate with the living. This was something Abigail Wincoff had wrestled with in the first few hours after her death.

Like a bolt of lightning from the sky, she suddenly understood what she needed to do. Her childish imagination had delivered, detail perfect, an ideal solution. An astral projection of her soul to perform the task of a ghostwriter emerged with a certain level of maturity to help her present her ideas effectively. Now her soul was in the shape of a young woman, fifteen years older. If only for a brief amount of time, she wanted to feel what it was like to be the woman she would have grown to be. Another thing she knew was that if she had lived, when she got to high school, she would have insisted the kids call her Gail. She had come to believe that if she watched closely, and with Gail, she could change the lives of those she loved and cared about.

She'd stared up at the ceiling trying to reconcile all the emotions running through her just before inserting a fresh sheet of paper into the typewriter. Suddenly, her shape wavered, dissolved, and then reshaped itself. It wasn't half as hard as she had thought astral projecting would be. But not without the occasional glitch.

The attic stairs were down. There was an unnatural chill in the air of the room, a lingering draft of rotting flesh. The photograph of Abigail Wincoff on a bicycle, which had been on the floor, had vanished — as if it had been a figment of the imagination. That was exactly what it had been. Such things inside Abby's imagined world served as a distraction from her unsettling thoughts and filled the void of her loneliness.

Her apparition was at the window, staring out into the woods as the darkness crept slowly over the landscape. All alone, waiting, sadness enveloped her in a tight hold.

"Little Bunny Foo Foo. Hopping through the forest," she sang meekly, her cheeks gleaming with ghostly tears.

Chapter 52

ON THE SECOND Wednesday of November, Sheriff Kirkman was in his office leaning back in his chair with his booted feet propped up on the corner of the desk. His eyes squinted, and forehead wrinkled in concentration as he thought about yesterday's election. It didn't bother him that Donald Trump would soon be in the White House. The local election was more important. He wasn't too keen on the sheriff that would be replacing him. From what he knew about the man, he was a tough Italian Catholic, short of stature, big of nose and worked like a Swiss watch: ordered, coldly methodical. He hadn't voted for him.

The sheriff swung his black boots off the desk, leaned forward in the seat, and sat there with a frown on his face. He thought about it some more. Then told himself now: *Wasn't his responsibility.* His job, which often involved handling traffic incidents, robberies, bar brawls and domestic fights, would soon be over. Despite that, he thought the newly elected sheriff wasn't all he was cracked up to be, he wasn't going to lose sleep over it.

His eyes turned to the stack of paperwork on his desk that needed his attention. Lately, he had gotten entirely too comfortable behind the desk. If he looked miserable, it was because he was wondering if he would ever be out on patrol again. It wasn't likely to happen. Or so he perhaps believed.

Thirty minutes hadn't even passed when he paused in his restless sorting through some papers. He looked at the clock, which told him it was nineteen minutes to eleven. That nagging desire to leave and go on patrol had been eating away at him. So, he punched his intercom button.

"Yes, Sheriff Kirkman?" Kimberly Kaasa answered.

"I'm going out for a while," he said, solemnly.

"When will you be back?"

"After lunchtime," he replied with authority, proud of the strong control he was exercising over his voice. "A couple of hours at most."

When almost an hour had gone by, and Kirkman was driving down the road in his Expedition, he felt the pangs of hunger. His early morning doughnuts had long since worn off, and his growling stomach couldn't be ignored.

He put his blinker on and turned around in a nearby driveway. As he drove with the intention to grab a bite to eat somewhere, something slammed into his mind. It was like a gust of wind — grateful that it struck his thoughts, not his body. The case of the missing and presumed dead, Abigail Wincoff. Maybe it was time to check in with the detective. About every ten days he made it a point to keep tabs on the case. He wanted to know if there were any developments, not only because Gillian Wincoff was still calling his office, but for his own peace of mind.

Later, in the office, Kirkman thought, *he'd phone Detective Silverwood and find out if there was any progress on the Abigail Wincoff case.*

Later came faster than he could imagine. That afternoon, in his office, not surprisingly, the detective had not taken his call. Right after he had returned to his paperwork. He was sifting through a stack of papers and wondering what happened to the stapler, when the phone rang.

"Sheriff Kirkman!" the jail commander exclaimed.

"Yes," the sheriff replied. "What do you have?"

"Half an hour ago, a prisoner, Casimiro Palacio, was found dead in his cell."

"Sorry to hear this news. What happened?" the sheriff prodded.

"Palacio had failed to answer the roll call. We found him lying on the floor inside his cell."

"Was he stabbed, or beaten up?" Kirkman asked in a rush.

There was a pause, a silence.

"No apparent wounds, no signs of foul play. He looks just like he's sleeping. But nobody moved him, so there might be something on his back. Still, I'm guessing it's likely to be either an overdose or natural causes, like a stroke or heart attack," the jail commander informed him.

A frown appeared on Kirkman's brow. The longer the jail commander kept talking, his frown lines became deeper. Nervously, he picked up a paper clip on his desk, held it on his palm, then started bending it back and forth.

"Is the jail locked down tight?" Kirkman asked.

"Yes, it sure is. It's a shame we have to do that."

"A dead prisoner is bad enough. The dispatcher will notify the medical examiner. I'll be right over," the sheriff said before he hung up and dropped the paper clip.

It then occurred to him that he would probably miss dinner. But he wouldn't mention it to his wife. Still, he didn't do well skipping meals. He hurried to the break room, opened the refrigerator, and helped himself to two doughnuts with white glazed icing and a can of diet coke. The same batch of doughnuts from this morning's briefing that weren't too stale.

It would have to do until dinner, he thought, before he proceeded to walk down the hall.

Now he was thinking about his retirement. Days like this, he wouldn't miss. So many times, he hadn't eaten properly or had skipped lunch entirely. But there were some things he would miss when he retired. Most especially, there were two things he liked participating in as the county's sheriff. He had enjoyed summers coaching Little League football on Saturdays and helping in the annual Christmas fundraiser for cystic fibrosis research.

The sound of the SUV starting up drew him out of his thoughts. Putting the Expedition in reverse and backing out of the parking lot, he focused on his present situation and drove for seven miles. As he turned onto Manor Drive, the new jail and communications center, built from hard-to come-by tax dollars, loomed in the distance.

A sudden burp reminded him of the slightly stale doughnuts and diet soda. *Something he shouldn't have eaten*, he thought.

Chapter 53

PEERING AROUND the doorjamb into the sheriff's office, Philip Silverwood rapped his knuckles against the door frame. At the sound, Kirkman's head whipped up and he saw the detective filling his doorway. The look Silverwood gave him indicated that his unannounced visit wasn't a spontaneous decision.

"I'm sorry we keep playing phone tag. Rather than call you back and leave a message again, I thought I'd stop by so we could talk," Silverwood said.

Kirkman gestured him in. Thereupon, Silverwood stepped into his office, and the sheriff came up out of his chair and shut the door. It wasn't long after the sheriff took a seat behind his desk that the talk drifted to the Abigail Wincoff case. After all the time that had gone by, the detective had no optimism about solving it.

It was now the first week of December, and still no sign of Abigail Wincoff. For a while longer, until the paper tore, Monroe County store owners kept her Missing Child flyer taped to the inside of their windows. Some gave the details to any customer who asked — young girl, woods, no body found.

The detective outlined the case, and the sheriff frowned, and asked, "Do you know what the real problem is?"

Silverwood hesitated, then took a deep breath and answered, "I suppose you're about to tell me."

"They tested the binoculars but didn't get any DNA and prints from them other than Abigail Wincoff's."

"This was a calculated crime. Many months, or even years of planning was involved by a cunning killer who had refined his methods. I don't think Abigail Wincoff was his first. That's why we're having such a hard time catching him. The only way to find Abigail Wincoff is to catch him," said the detective.

That part of the conversation had the sheriff thinking of all sorts of things. In addition, Kirkman didn't want the shame of a failed investigation. He just had not found the right clue. Which left him with a deep-seated yearning to find that one breakthrough.

With all that on his mind, the sheriff chewed his lip for a couple of seconds, then looked up. "Supposing you're right about this killer. That she wasn't kidnapped or trafficked. Perhaps my original assumption was correct. That she was murdered by a traveling serial killer. It's a reality I've struggled with all along."

"It's a sad reality that we have to face. The out-and-out truth is, we're never going to find her body," Detective Silverwood said with some reluctance.

It had been around three months since Abigail Wincoff went missing. They weren't any closer to knowing what had happened to her. The case was going cold. The police department had neither the budget nor the time to keep investigating a case that refused to yield anything new. It was Silverwood's job to make certain the unsolved cases went into a storage box, permitting the department's resources to be allocated elsewhere.

The detective wiped a hand across his mouth before he said, "You and I both know what having no leads, no witnesses and nothing left to follow up on is like. The case is going nowhere. Maybe it is better to leave it alone."

Kirkman's nostrils flared as he jerked up in the chair and gripped the armrest, his knuckles turning white.

A second or so later, the sheriff paced around his office, a knuckle pressed to his lips. "Would you like me to excuse myself from the case?"

Silverwood was going to have his say, every word of it. "I'm not telling you to give up. Look, I'm the central clearinghouse. I know what's best for this case. What I'm telling you is the case just can't be solv —"

"You think I've been in the job too long?" the sheriff interrupted roughly.

Detective Silverwood's voice was cold, his eyes skeptical, speculative. "That's … coming out of left field. But maybe so. I know you don't want to hear that, and I don't like telling you. Besides, it doesn't matter one way or another since you're retiring next month."

Kirkman's mouth closed in a grim line. He was visibly upset at the reminder — his posture had changed, and his brow wrinkled.

"What else can I say? It's not the easiest thing to do, to see a case like this end up with no closure. That's the reason I'm here telling you because I just wanted to give you a heads-up. I know how attached you are to this case," Silverwood added when he didn't say anything.

Fists on his hips, the sheriff felt tension sizzling through his body. He wanted to argue but held himself back, knowing there was no point. Silverwood was right on all accounts. In all actuality, the detective's words were a cold slap of reality.

Sheriff Kirkman lowered his arms to his sides, his body language softening. Though his tirade had ended, his fleeting thoughts were unsettled by the tension between them.

After another moment had passed, they took their original positions. The sheriff sat behind the desk and Silverwood sat in front of it. They talked about the case for the next twenty minutes. After that, the sheriff lingered for a bit, as if waiting for something more and Silverwood's patience ran out.

In a most abrupt way, the detective excused himself. He nodded in a businesslike way to the sheriff before twisting the knob on the door and walking out.

Kirkman stormed around his desk, slammed the door shut, and then collapsed into his chair. Jaw clenched, he leaned forward, resting his elbows on the desk, the chair squeaking loudly. Tension still gripped him. He closed his eyes and rubbed his temples with his thumbs. Feeling hot under the collar, he could do with some fresh air. Since it was already approaching noon, this seemed to him like a good time to take a lunch break. And he already knew where he wanted to go.

Chapter 54

AS THE SHERIFF turned into the parking lot of the Victoria Station restaurant, he was thinking about the last bit of the conversation he'd had with Detective Silverwood. The main problem was, a part of him didn't want to accept that the Abigail Wincoff case couldn't be solved. *Perhaps after a good meal he could think of something to move the case forward,* he thought as he eased into a parking space and cut the engine of his Expedition. He believed that his mind worked better on a full stomach.

When he walked into the restaurant, the maître d' welcomed him with enthusiasm and sat him at a table. Estelle Rowland noticed him, stepped into the kitchen, and grabbed a pot of coffee.

Automatically, she went to his table, poured him a mug of coffee, and offered cream and sugar, both of which he accepted.

"Long time no see, Andy. I've got some news. Starting in January, I'm only going to be working here part-time. Due to retire soon," she said, clutching the coffee pot to her bosom.

Sighing, he said, "You and me both, Estelle. I'll be out of office in January, the same day as the inauguration of the new president."

"Donald Trump, can you believe it? Don't blame me — I didn't vote for him."

"I didn't think you had. He doesn't seem like your kind of guy," he said and frowned.

Something suddenly occurred to her. Her eyes shot to the Missing Child flyer on the wall by the entrance. For a minute, she kept staring, gripping the coffee pot even more tightly. Emotions shifted inside her. She turned her eyes toward the sheriff and went right into it.

"This is the exact table where he had sat. That can't be a coincidence."

"Who are you talking about, Estelle?"

"I'm talking about the man I had waited on just before that girl disappeared. Pedophile. Child molester. At the time, that's what I thought he was," she said out of the side of her mouth, eyes narrowed, face scrunched up.

Estelle saw the surprised look on his face when she said it, but she had to say it.

"What makes you say such things? Sounds like you didn't care for him," he pressed, shot a sideways glance at her, and set the menu aside.

It seemed clear there was more to come, he thought, knowing she was working herself up to what she really wanted to say. He clasped his hands in front of him and studied her expectant expression.

"Personally, I didn't. But that's neither here nor there," Estelle tacked on with a laugh, then pursed her lips in disapproval.

His one-word response came a second later: Okay.

She paused for a moment to gather her thoughts, took a breath, and let it all pour out. "There was something wrong about the way he was looking at that little girl who was sitting at a table with her parents. He stared at her with such intensity, like she was his for the taking. Then she was gone, and he was gone. He could have abducted her."

"Could be a coincidence," Kirkman interjected.

"You're the sheriff."

"And that means what?" he had to ask.

"You're not supposed to believe in coincidences," Estelle said with a raised eyebrow.

Kirkman gave her a squint-eyed look. "Just to confirm we're on the same page. You're talking about Abigail Wincoff. The girl on that Missing Child flyer pinned on the corkboard over there?"

"You betcha. She had been here with her parents, just before she vanished. I apologize for not finding you and telling you my suspicions sooner. For a while I wasn't sure that I should say anything. I was worried you would think I'm neurotic. Then I completely forgot. My memory isn't what it used to be. Seeing you here, sitting at this table, I remembered again. And, I thought, What the heck? I may as well tell you."

"Is there anything else you'd like to add, before I order lunch?"

"Well, I never found out his name. But I think it's weird that his red Chevy pickup was dusty, as if it had traveled a long distance. Yet it had Maryland plates. So, I wrote the license number on a napkin, and I have kept it folded in my wallet ever since. Hereafter, I'll leave the investigating to you."

An alarm bell went off in his mind. He remembered the case file. His mind was computer-like in its ability to store information. In a way, what Estelle said supported the maid's statement. The maid had reported seeing a red pickup truck driven by a careless driver on Sellersville Drive.

The sheriff reached inside his coat and pulled a small notepad out of his shirt pocket and handed it to her along with a pen. "I'd be very obliged if you'd write down the make, color and model of his truck, and the license plate number, Estelle. And write down everything you can remember about him. His hair color, how tall he was, what he was wearing."

"Tell me what you're having first. I'll take the order to the kitchen. Then I'll write it all down."

"Sounds good to me. I'll have the brisket platter with cheesy scalloped potatoes, salad, and a large coke."

Lunch came and went. The sheriff left the restaurant, a little heavier, and a little optimistic. Whistling to himself in the parking lot, he moved at a fast pace toward his SUV.

While driving, he forced himself to review everything he knew about the Abigail Wincoff case. If he could establish a connection between Abby and the man Estelle Rowland had described, then he would have a lead on the killer — assuming he was the killer.

Chapter 55

IMMEDIATELY after stepping into his office, the sheriff found himself digging through a file box on the bookcase. He couldn't leave it alone, couldn't stop thinking about what Estelle Rowland had said. He grabbed the file on Abigail Wincoff, set it down on the desk and stared at it. A sense of duty washed over him in a wave. He committed himself to Abigail Wincoff. It wasn't for Detective Silverwood to advise him to toss this case aside, just because he was the lead.

He slumped into the chair behind his desk and began thumbing through the contents: an informal photograph of Abigail Wincoff smiling outside her New Jersey house, a couple of dozen digital prints of the cabin she'd been staying at with her parents and the area around it. His reports were in chronological order. He hadn't written much either.

His hands pulled out Millie Dozier's statement to Deputy Missy Sparks. Reading it over, he was glad to confirm that she mentioned she'd almost been driven off Sellersville Drive by a red pickup truck. That couldn't be a coincidence. Estelle was right to point out that he didn't believe in coincidences.

"This could be the start of something," he said quietly to himself.

Rather, it seemed to him, it was more like the killer was fleeing the scene of the murder at the same time Millie was driving on the road toward the cabin. The very cabin he had broken into and washed his hands of Abigail Wincoff's blood.

That was when he fidgeted about in his jacket pocket and pulled out his notepad. He flipped it open to the page, where Estelle had written down the suspicious man's license plate number. He pushed the intercom for Kimberly and asked her to run the plate number. It wasn't but a couple of minutes later Kimberly told him that license plate was reported stolen.

Then he picked up the phone and called Detective Silverwood. His office number rang three times before it went to voicemail. He left him a message telling him there was a new development on the Abigail Wincoff case. After hanging up, he placed Estelle's handwritten notes into the case file.

Still, there was a dilemma: Abby was presumed dead, but they hadn't found her body. There was no hard evidence that she'd been killed.

Another thing that troubled him was how he had trouble determining the exact time of her disappearance. It was presumed Abby left the cabin, alone, after having breakfast with her mother, at 9:40 Tuesday morning and hadn't returned. Only that much was clear.

Now what? he thought, as he sifted through the stack of Missing Child flyers. He had memorized Abby's face, but he looked at them anyway.

Adamantly, he went back to studying the case file for what seemed like a long time. He had interviewed more than a dozen people including Abigail Wincoff's mother and father, Joy Franklin, the cabin's rental agent, and the staff of the Clean As A Whistle cleaning service. Gillian Wincoff had been questioned twice. He had extracted narratives of their knowledge of Abby and an account of their whereabouts on Tuesday, August 23, the day she went missing.

Heavy thoughts pressed against his mind. Had he missed something important? Had the search been conducted properly? These and other questions ran through his mind as he put the papers back into the folder. And it frustrated him because he just didn't have the answers. He closed up the file and shoved it over to the side. Even though he knew he had done his best, his best just hadn't cut it. Well, that was how he felt.

It was the end of the day. His fact-finding would have to wait another day. More waiting on a case that was going cold fast. The one the detective had said couldn't be solved. With that thought, he felt his temper surging its way through him, demanding an outlet. So, he decided he better go because that line of thinking wasn't going to do him any good.

He tossed the Abigail Wincoff case file back into the box on the bookcase. He shook the anguish out of his mind but was still lost in thought when he slipped around his desk and walked out of the office. And when he passed Livengood in the lobby, he barely noticed him standing there. The chief deputy bid him a goodnight and he responded with a grunt and a nod before he walked out the door.

The sheriff was still brooding as he stepped outside. It was cold, drizzling and almost fully dark. A sharp wind whistled through the parking lot. He winced from it, his eyes small slits. Without haste, he turned his back against the wind and moved swiftly toward his Monroe County Sheriff's Department issued vehicle.

Once inside his Expedition, he rubbed his eyes, then fired up the engine. His dashboard clock read 6:38. He backed out of the parking area and drove away without so much as a backward glance. Sulking, he began the journey to his house.

Minutes into the drive, he noticed the weather taking a turn for the worse. He watched through the windshield as the thick clouds smudged with shades of gray increased in intensity as the drizzle turned into rain. Droplets of water smeared down the glass as he turned on the wipers.

Kirkman had to snap out of his mood. With a bit of effort, he pushed the darker thoughts out of his head and concentrated on traveling on the slippery roads. Under such circumstances, it was the sensible thing to do.

In spite, all his effort produced no real gain. The gloomy atmosphere didn't lift his spirits any.

Chapter 56

SLOWLY Kristi Maratos awoke in her cozy townhouse in Nesquehoning. She opened her eyes at the first sign of morning sunlight streaming through the half-opened crocheted lace curtains that hung over the window. Before she could get her bearings the cell phone on the nightstand rang. For the next twelve minutes, she was lying on her bed, talking to Billy Shipley on her cell phone.

After the call ended, she stared at her phone until the screen locked and went black. During that time, she'd been thinking how they were getting along well. Over the short time they had known each other they had established an amazing rapport.

Despite still feeling tired, she left the bed with a smile as she dragged her hand self-consciously through her tangled hair. She was pressed for time, due to appear on camera at 7:30 A.M. to anchor the morning news show on BRC TV13.

After her shower, she dressed quickly and stepped out into the bitterly cold morning. With the sun shining out of a blue, cloudless sky, she drove out into the countryside in her Mazda sedan. The roads were clear all the way to Lehighton.

The very second she stepped through the door of the station, her regular cameraman, Morris Miller, saw her and called her over to him.

She frowned impatiently, and he beckoned more insistently. "Come look at this video."

"This better be good. I'm on in fifteen minutes," she said as she joined him in the control room overlooking the news studio.

"Let me cue up the video footage," he said, and sat in a chair in front of a control board and bank of monitors.

He rewound slowly, stopping on a clean shot of the sunlight reflecting on a little girl, running in the woods. Then he pressed play.

"You want to explain to me why I just saw Abigail Wincoff, alive and in color?" Kristi asked, shock rippling through her.

The cameraman had shot the B-roll footage of the woods surrounding the Wincoff's rental cabin for the story about their missing daughter on that Friday in August. The video was excellent and graphic.

"Yeah, that looks like the missing girl. That's why I wanted you to see it. I can't believe I didn't catch this before. Late yesterday afternoon I was screening footage from the field for the archives when I saw it," he said with bright enthusiasm.

"This is weird. From what I could see, she was dressed the same way, and carrying a doll," she added.

"What should I do?" he asked.

"After the broadcast, I'll call Deputy Shipley to come have a look. He'll know what to do," she suggested.

"Kristi, that's a good idea. Until later, then."

When Kristi called the deputy with news of a possible sighting of Abigail Wincoff, he showed up at the station during his lunch break. They watched the footage through once. Then Morris leapt out of his seat and moved to the side of the screen, and he pointed at the reflection of what appeared to be a girl.

Running the footage through his brain, Shipley simply couldn't believe his eyes and asked to see it again. Morris returned to the mouse. The footage rewound, stopped with a jerk, then played at a slower speed.

The deputy watched for a while, then turned away. "It's not her."

Kristi and Morris looked at each other with confused expressions.

"It's a little girl, wearing a white dress and holding a doll, fitting her description," Kristi insisted to him.

Shipley frowned down at the monitor. "The image wasn't clear at all. It could be anyone. More likely a member of the forensic team in a white Tyvek suit, carrying equipment."

"But, that's not what I see!" Morris said, his gay voice suddenly serious.

Eyebrows rose and defiant looks were exchanged. *This was not good*, Kristi thought.

"It's not Abigail Wincoff," Shipley said in a loud voice, then took a breath, and said in a reasonable tone. "I know you'd both like it to be her. I want it to be her. But I know it's not her, because I was there that day along with many police officers. If there had been a girl running through the woods, someone would have seen her, right?"

Aware of the sudden tension in the control room, Kristi, with careful consideration, thought more about what he'd said. With misty eyes, she nodded, agreeing with him.

"Now that you put it that way, I see that it makes sense. Somebody would've seen her for sure. Nobody saw her. And that could only mean that she couldn't have been there. Whatever or whoever that is captured on the video, isn't her," she said, and sent a glance at Morris over her shoulder then shook her hair.

"Do you have any more footage?" Shipley asked him.

"No, this is it," Morris told him, then he jerked his head away, returning his attention to the monitor.

"I'm sorry for wasting your time," Kristi said blankly.

"Don't say that, baby. You could never waste my time. I'm glad you let me know. I'd be failing in my duty as a deputy if I didn't follow up on any possible lead that might assist in tracking down the whereabouts of Abigail Wincoff," Shipley explained kindly.

It wasn't so much what he said, but the way that he said it, his eyes holding hers, the sincerity in his words endearing him to her. That made her feel better about everything.

"I'll make a copy of the footage, and store it, in case you want to refer to it again sometime in the future," Morris interrupted their moment.

"That won't be necessary. But do it if it makes you feel better," Shipley said to him, then turned to her. "Anyway, I have to get back. I'll call you later."

She gave Shipley a reassuring smile and kissed his cheek before he left the room. What else could she do?

Chapter 57

SLUGGISHLY, Sheriff Kirkman walked into his office, hugging his stomach. He wished now he hadn't had that breakfast. His stomach churned. And his face contorted with discomfort. He had just come from the bathroom, and he hoped he wouldn't have to go there again.

He fell into his chair, doing his best not to feel the way his stomach lurched. The chair creaked as he leaned forward a little, trying to get somewhat comfortable. He reached into a desk drawer, hunting for the roll of antacid tablets. He located the package and popped two in his mouth before closing his eyes. As if in a meditative state, he concentrated on keeping his stomach settled.

Now, feeling more relaxed and comfortable, he opened his eyes to see a stack of mail and papers on his desk. He opened his desk drawer and extracted his silver letter opener and began applying it to the stack of envelopes.

Sometime after ten A.M., Kimberly Kaasa handed him a faxed copy of the medical examiner's autopsy results on Casimiro Palacio. That, along with the interviews conducted by Deputy Shipley and Deputy Sparks with each of Palacio's former cellmates. The medical examiner's report indicated Palacio had died of natural causes. He'd had a stroke brought on by a heart condition. This evidence exonerated Andy Kirkman's department from blame regarding Palacio's death. But he knew from bitter experience that what seemed plain as day to him, wouldn't satisfy any family members left behind willing to file a wrongful-death claim, something that happened often when an inmate died.

It couldn't have been more than a second or two when his intercom buzzed, jolting him from his thoughts. He set the fax on the desk and listened to Kimberly Kaasa inform him that he had a call from Gillian Wincoff. Hesitantly, he accepted her call. And just that fast, the Abigail Wincoff case came roaring into his mind. He told her he couldn't go into detail, but there was a possible lead. He hadn't heard anything definite about the suspect driving a vehicle with a stolen license plate spotted in the vicinity at the time of the disappearance from Detective Silverwood. If anything, the news of a lead gave her the impression that he hadn't given up on finding out what happened to her daughter.

After the call, he found himself brooding about what he could or couldn't do for the next hour. One thing he knew for sure was that he wasn't in the mood to call Detective Silverwood. It was just days ago, it seemed, that he'd talked to him at great length about the possible suspect in the case. He reclined back in his chair and thought about the suspect the detective had called "a person of interest wanted for questioning" in the investigation of Abigail Wincoff's disappearance.

With all the time that had gone by, he had to ask himself: Was it worth checking out the area around the cabin on Wagon Trail Road? Yes, he decided he would do it. Only God knew why! Perhaps he was drawn to the cabin by a morbid kind of curiosity, knowing the killer had been there. The intense expression on his face tightened on that thought.

A part of him felt like he was wasting his time. Yet another part of him was urging him to go. Something inside him wouldn't let him give up.

Kirkman sighed a long sigh as he stood from his chair and prayed his stomach would not erupt. He put on his jacket and hat and left the office.

The air outside was brisk, the temperature cold. The sky was overcast with clouds. He hurried over to his SUV.

Roughly twenty minutes later he had reached Wagon Trail Road. The road was slick with hidden patches of ice, so he had to drive more carefully. He began to wonder if he had made the right decision. Why in God's name had he made the drive over?

When he passed a gap in the of trees, something caught his eye, something that made him slow down, hit the brakes, and stare. The Expedition's engine idled in a soft, low purr while he watched a little girl walk into the middle of the road. She had on a simple white dress and her feet were bare. For a fleeting second, she looked in his direction, and he saw that her eyes were black. And then she disappeared into the trees.

What was she doing out here alone? he thought.

After a beat or so, he drove forward. As he neared the spot where he'd seen the girl standing, he leaned over the steering wheel and peered into the woods. He looked in every direction but didn't see her. Then he faced forward, drove on and gave it no more thought.

There was a FOR SALE sign on the property. The owner had put the cabin on the market. In the last year, renters had been few and far between. If you thought about it, the place was bad luck and best avoided. This was all because Abigail Wincoff's blood had been found in the kitchen sink. The cabin had been unoccupied ever since. Unless you count the maids from the Clean As A Whistle cleaning service.

The sheriff passed between two trees, pulled into the driveway, and backed the Expedition beside the cabin.

He stayed sitting in the SUV, long after he turned off the ignition. It was quiet enough that he could hear the wind in the trees and the ping under his SUV as the engine cooled. A knot in his stomach twisted the moment he looked in the direction of the cabin. The Abigail Wincoff case had left him with a bad taste in his mouth when it came to that place.

"If there was such a thing as a haunted place, it was that cabin," he whispered to himself.

Kirkman wasn't sure what made him say that just then. He could only assume it was because the cabin looked so desolate. How could he know that the ghost of Abigail Wincoff was watching him from the attic window? When by chance he looked in her direction, she retreated before he could see her. If, in fact, he was able to see her at all.

Chapter 58

THE INSTANT Sheriff Kirkman stepped out of his Ford Expedition; a blast of cold air blew straight at him. He hunched against it and raised the collar of his Monroe County Sheriff's Department tan parka, complete with a gold star on his chest. It seemed like he'd forgotten what true cold felt like in Pennsylvania in December.

This wintry morning, he walked around the cabin, eyes narrowed against the wind. Momentarily, he looked at the rear wall of the cabin. Whoosh! came the wind, blowing through the nearby trees, kicking up leaves and swirling them around.

As he approached the front of the cabin, he noticed the front door was opened a crack. He reasoned that the gusts of wind might have pushed it open. Or it could be a break-in. What were the chances it would happen again? Anyhow, he decided to investigate.

He ducked low, his hand resting on the butt of the Glock holstered on his hip. The howling wind grew louder and swirled around him as he stepped closer to the door. Peering through a window, he couldn't see so much as a shadow. Still, he wanted to search, thinking there might be an intruder.

After stepping inside, he noticed it was colder than he expected, but at least he was sheltered from the wind. A quick glance around told him that, there weren't any windows open.

Moving with quiet caution, he worked his way through the entire cabin, skipping the attic and basement. The silence was omnipresent, punctuated by an occasional creak in the floor. Filled with nervous energy, he checked doors and windows, making certain everything was secure.

Nothing seemed out of place — or so, he had thought.

In the bathroom, he walked over to the sink and ran the faucet to wash his hands. The water ran brown with dirt.

He was on his way out the door when his eyes stopped on something in the corner of the room. His brows drew together in a sharp winging angle as he tried to puzzle it out. There stood a table with a typewriter upon it and beside it was a manuscript. A manuscript?

"How did that get there?" he asked himself aloud.

The sheriff had to walk over and take a look. For a brief interval, he stood by the table and stared at the mysterious manuscript titled *Murder in the Poconos* with an intensity that made the hair on the back of his neck stand up. Thinking back over the years as a sheriff, he had seen many strange things, but this was one of the strangest things he'd ever seen.

A branch scraped against the living room window, and he jumped. His heart racing as he slowly looked over his shoulder. Nothing. No face stared back at him from the semi-darkness. And the only sound was the wind outside.

Should he touch the manuscript? Was it evidence? Just in case, he took a pair of gloves from his SUV. Although his hands were steady when he pulled the gloves on, underneath his fingertips he could feel his pulse throb. Even with his parka, the wind was unbearable.

His expression turned into one of disbelief as he picked up the manuscript. The author's name was on the title page: Gail Wincoff. Something he had failed to notice earlier. A million questions were spinning through his head. Who was she? Was she related to Abigail Wincoff? Was this some kind of sick joke? Could it be a calling card left behind by the killer? That would explain the break-in.

His attention was focused on the manuscript, but he was also making occasional glances over his shoulder. He hoped he could catch whoever it was that put the manuscript there.

What he didn't see was the ghost of Abigail Wincoff. She was lurking by the armrest of the couch. She'd been watching him the entire time.

He took the manuscript to the couch with him and examined the pages, which were typed. Rather than read it word for word, he skimmed through it. He just wanted to know what it was about.

Suddenly he felt a presence. Was somebody there? he wondered. He gave the room a quick glance, but nothing caught his eye. Then he returned to skimming the manuscript.

He read the words by the girl whose ghostly presence, now hovered at his shoulder. "My surname was Wincoff, first name Abigail. I was twelve when I was murdered on August 23, 2016."

At the mention of her name, an electric shock seemed to zip through his body. The answers to her disappearance were there in black and white.

"My murderer was a man fueled by rage. I don't know where he came from. What I do know is that he is a serial killer."

As he turned the pages, he felt like Abigail Wincoff was with him. But the feeling vanished as quickly as it had come.

A sense of relief fell over Abby as she watched him read the manuscript. And best of all, her pain was slipping away, seeping into the ground beneath her. Would her soul be at peace now? All this time she had hoped.

Was closure for her family, not enough?

Unfortunately, there was too much uncertainty stirring inside her. Try as she might, trying to force the memory of her murder away, she couldn't block out the images. How could she ever be happy again?

Her spirit vanished from the room.

There came a familiar sound against the windows, a sound the sheriff knew well. Now, he was worried about the weather. He went to the nearest window on the adjacent wall, which had the curtains drawn open, and looked out. The snow was coming down fast and hard, in thick white sheets.

So, without further delay, he pushed the manuscript inside his parka and moved toward the front door. When he yanked the door open, a swirl of snow blew in and pelted his face.

Chapter 59

AT TWO MINUTES past twelve, in the midst of a snowstorm, the BRC TV13 news crew was set up on the sidewalk of Analomink Street in East Stroudsburg. Kristi Maratos turned to the camera. Her leather-gloved hands held a microphone up to her mouth and gave a nod at the cameraman, Morris Miller, who adjusted the eyepiece.

Over a mile away, in the Monroe County Sheriff's Office, Chief Deputy Livengood set about making himself a coffee in the break room. As it often was, a large flat-screen television mounted on the wall was turned on. Across the bottom of the screen were the words: NEWS13 SPECIAL REPORT — WEATHER EMERGENCY.

A reporter came into view standing outside in the snow.

"We take you to Kristi Maratos, on the scene at the East Stroudsburg Municipal Building. Kristi, what can you tell us?" came an announcer's voice.

Hearing that made Livengood turn to watch the television.

With a smirk on his face, he called from the doorway of the room. "Shipley! Get in here. Your girlfriend is on TV."

Deputy Shipley was in Kimberly's cubicle, speaking to her about an incident that had happened earlier.

"Kimberly, if you'll excuse me. It would probably be in my best interest to find out what the Chief Deputy is talking about," he said, and walked away.

"You go right ahead," she said with a slightly aloof look on her face.

Shipley came into the break room and stared at the TV where Kristi Maratos, dressed in a heavy wool coat over business attire, was talking. His heart was pitter-pattering as he watched her.

"As you can see behind me, the streets are deserted except for emergency vehicles. The storm has just begun. Just in the last hour, about a foot of snow has already fallen. East Stroudsburg is supposed to get another six inches by nightfall," she said, hovering, snow falling behind her.

The camera cut to the street where heavy snow was falling. Shipley was ready to talk.

"So, let's get this right. I'm just seeing her, that's all. She's just a friend. She's not my girlfriend," he corrected the Chief Deputy.

"Sure, she's not. I know you're only thirty. No reason to commit. I only thought she was different," Livengood teased.

"She is. I really like her. I'm just taking my time with it. If it's meant to be, it'll be. Let's watch TV, okay?" Shipley said and turned his attention to the television.

The screen changed and Kristi Maratos assumed a serious face and began talking to the camera. "Severe storm warnings are in effect from Pennsylvania to western Maryland. Flight cancellations and even three-to-four-hour delays are to be expected at the airports. Pennsylvania's governor strongly advises the public to stay in their homes until the storm subsides."

When the commercials came on, Livengood left the room only to return a minute later.

"By the way, Kimberly wants to talk to you, so don't keep her waiting too long. Apparently you have unfinished business that needs to be addressed," the chief deputy reminded him, then stepped out of the room.

Before leaving the room, Shipley glanced back to see Kristi one more time, but the commercials were still running. For just an instant his face showed disappointment with eyes expressing unguarded emotion. He turned his head forward and exited the room, adjusting his duty belt as he walked toward the dispatcher's cubicle.

Meanwhile, in East Stroudsburg, Kristi's body visibly shook from the cold. She was eager for the commercial break to end.

Morris nodded, the camera's red light winking on, and she gave her closing comments. "I'm sorry to be the bearer of bad news, but I'm afraid we're in for quite a lot of snow. Things will get worse before they get better. This is Kristi

Maratos reporting outside the East Stroudsburg Municipal Building. Back to the newsroom."

The live broadcast was over. Briefly Kristi ran her hands through her hair to shake off the snowflakes that had blown in her direction. In the short time she'd been there, the wind lifted from twenty to twenty-five knots. Snow slanted down now, and visibility was dwindling.

The snow swirled viciously about her, and she turned away from it, facing the street. She heard a vehicle's tires crunch in the snow and looked in the direction of the noise. By squinting against the snow blowing into her face she could see Sheriff Kirkman's Expedition. The snow was blurring the windshield of his SUV, much too fast for the wipers to clear it away.

The sheriff's SUV rolled to a stop at a traffic light on the corner. As soon as the light changed, Kirkman briefly glanced her way. Their eyes met briefly before he looked back at the road and drove on. In the span of those few seconds, she wondered what the soon-to-retire sheriff was thinking.

Kristi sighed. She watched her breath fogging in the cold air. Then she turned around and handed the microphone to the engineer guy, which he took and placed it inside the news van.

"We need to get a move on. I don't want to get stuck in this," she said as she walked over to Morris.

He said something to the engineer guy, who was sitting inside the back of the van before he slammed the back door and said, "I hear you, Kristi. Let's get rolling."

Kristi slid into the passenger's side, and Morris slid into the driver's side. The van's engine roared to life, then sped off and disappeared down the street. The picturesque view of the falling snow and the snow layering the empty streets with white made a dismal scene.

Chapter 60

THE ATTIC WINDOW rattled with a sudden gust of wind that had hurled snow pellets against the glass. The ghost of Abby drifted by the window, her restless soul stirring. She'd been staring out the window long after watching Sheriff Andy Kirkman's vehicle drive away. The discovery of her manuscript, *Murder in the Poconos,* by the sheriff did not give her the sense of closure she had hoped for. Though for her parents, closure would come. They would learn what had happened to her. And her body would be exhumed from beneath the cabin for burial. Would she ever see her parents again? She hoped but didn't know how it was possible.

But none of that mattered to her now because she was dead. She didn't want to be dead. And she couldn't understand why she had to die.

Her soul wasn't at peace.

She brought the doll to her chest, and this comforted her. It was something she often did when she'd been alive.

Her spirit left the window and the attic and drifted to the living room, returning to the window. The wind and snow pounded against the glass and snow was piled on the sill. And the falling snow blocked her view of the woods.

Abby couldn't feel the cold but was no stranger to snow. Growing up in New Jersey, she had gotten used to snow. It was a stunning phenomenon. Or so she thought when she was alive. Now in a spiritual state, the snow didn't faze her one bit.

The cabin had become her home. She was tied to the place her killer had laid her to rest. Forever? That she didn't know. Time made no sense to her. The days and nights seemed as one. And it was easy to lose track of the time.

Tormented by an insatiable hunger for answers, a swarm of questions clouded her thoughts. What was her next move? Would her soul cross over? Where would she go? Until now, her own mortality was something she'd never thought about. And she couldn't sort it out.

During this moment of soul searching the most magical thing happened. A light appeared to her, trickling in through the living room window. Was it the path to eternal happiness? After all, she was an innocent soul, lost and confused, too young to understand.

As the light grew larger, she was unsure of what it was and where it would lead her. Even though she felt a warmth all through her, as if all the love she wanted was there, in that light.

Was it a doorway to heaven?

Surely, she was eligible to enter the kingdom of Heaven. This was her choice, and hers alone. And she recognized that this was her chance to enter a better world for all eternity. Her spirit tried to focus on how good the light felt, and not the turmoil in her soul.

But she didn't want to leave the living world.

In a split second, her spirit backpedaled away from the light, and moved to the other side of the room. She turned around, her back facing the light, shielding herself from its rays. Her decision was made: she would remain with the living, like a spectator on the sidelines of life. Here on earth, she could watch the sunrise and see the birds whenever she wanted to. She might even imagine more projections of herself to play with.

The light was leaving the room, slowly, as if giving her a chance to reconsider. But she didn't relent. She wouldn't turn around until she was sure the light was long gone.

Now it was darker than the darkness of the living room.

Out of the dark came a shape then a deep, throaty hiss. Abby's soul didn't stir. Darkness crept all around her, came into her. She felt sudden rage boiling within her. The resentment of losing her life festered deep inside. She wanted to feel it. Needed to feel it.

There was something else stirring inside her: something evil and hard to ignore. It felt like she was being eaten alive. The rage was devouring her, changing her, overtaking her soul. What was happening to her?

But there was no fear in her. She didn't try to escape. Rather she gave herself utterly to whatever it was.

Her spirit turned around and lifted into the air. Floating in mid-air, she spun aimlessly, slowly.

As she fell to the floor, her image was tilted at an angle. In a few movements, her image jerked itself straight, still holding her doll. Within a minute's time, she changed from a child with soft features and paper-pale skin to a rotting corpse, in a state of yellow and green decay.

The ghost of Abigail Wincoff turned around to face the hallway, reddish eyes staring blankly out of her ghastly face. The doll slipped from her hand to the floor. A deep, throaty moan escaped from within her. She drifted forward, stepped on the doll, as if it meant nothing to her, just before it vanished.

As she traveled down the hall, she sang off key. "Little Bunny Foo Foo, Little Bunny Foo Foo. Hopping through the forest."

Something in her voice was different — raspy and low. She stopped in front of the door that led to the basement. A sinister laugh came from her before she — disappeared.

There was a long silence, punctuated by whispers. Just minutes later a low moaning sound filled the air.

But no sign of Abby.

The moaning and whispering ceased. The only sound that came was that of the whine and snarl of the wind which flung the snow against the windows.

"Gail, where are you? Please come and play with me. I don't want to play alone," came a loud, harsh, and demon-like voice that vibrated through the cabin.

Epilogue

THE KNOCK on the door startled Lance Wincoff, who had been spending a lazy Saturday in the living room, reading the paper. To his surprise it was Detective Philip Silverwood outside the front door, on the porch. It seemed there was a new development in the disappearance of his daughter.

"I would have called, but this kind of news should be delivered in person. I owe you that much at least," the detective said as he walked into the living room.

Gillian Wincoff, dressed in a baggy sweatshirt and jeans bolted into the living room. "Honey, who's there?"

Her hair was damp, like she'd just come out of the shower. Before Lance could answer her, a frazzled Gillian watched the detective escorted to the loveseat in the living room.

"Good morning, Mrs. Wincoff," Silverwood greeted her formally.

Lance, dressed in pajamas and a dark blue woolen bathrobe, gestured to the sofa. "Have a seat, dear. The detective has some news for us."

A chill ran through her veins. Her intuition kicked in. She knew — she just knew — that it wasn't good news. She braced herself emotionally.

"I'm fine standing," she said to her husband, then turned to the detective, and asked, "Did you find her?"

She sensed in her heart what he was going to say, but she couldn't stop herself from asking.

"The day after a snowstorm, a body had been exhumed from beneath a cabin on Wagon Trail Road in East Stroudsburg. Late last night I was at the morgue to witness the Monroe County Coroner make a positive identification. I hate to tell you this, but it is Abby."

"Are you telling me my Abby is dead?" she asked as if she hadn't heard him correctly.

"Yes, she is. I'm sorry. DNA confirmed it. As you are well aware, DNA samples had been taken of your daughter and inputted into CODIS. The blow fly larvae specimens collected from Abby's eyes, and from all appearances, indicate that she had died on the day of her disappearance," Silverwood explained to her.

With utter incomprehension, she opened her mouth in a silent scream, then buried her face in her hands. Noisy sobs followed. Who killed Abby? Why would someone kill a child? So many questions raced through her head.

Silverwood had tried to be tactful, but there was no way to soften the blow. Looking at her weary, grief-ravaged face, he could feel the pain she felt. He sympathized with her and stayed quiet for a few moments, giving her time to regain her composure.

Lance's eyes were vacant, until tears welled up. Gillian all but collapsed on the sofa. He threw his arm around his wife's shoulders, pulled her close to his side, too stunned by it all to do much of anything but listen.

The detective continued telling them that Sheriff Andy Kirkman had found a manuscript for a novel that was essentially about the killing of their daughter. Sure, enough Abby was buried in the place described in the manuscript. The police came to the conclusion that the killer had typed it and put it in the cabin on Wagon Trail Road to taunt the police. No fingerprints were found on the manuscript or the typewriter.

Furthermore, the detective said to them, "Often serial killers tend to leave a calling card behind at the crime scene. This manuscript about your daughter Abby is just some sick game the killer is playing."

"Serial killer?" Gillian mumbled aloud.

Of all the things Detective Silverwood knew for sure, it was that there was a serial killer on the loose, preying on young girls. The police were baffled and thought the manuscript was a strange calling card from the killer. Did he want to be caught and stopped? Was he a calculating murderer who craved notoriety for his killings?

"Did you visit a popular Stroudsburg restaurant called Victoria Station with Abby before her disappearance?" the detective inquired.

This question gave them something else to think about.

"Yes. We had gone there for lunch. If I'm not mistaken, it was the day before she vanished," Lance said, a little dumfounded.

"We've got a lead on an unidentified suspect that remains at large. A witness provided a description of a man who was gawking at your daughter in Victoria Station. By some strange coincidence, her description of him matches, right down to the last detail, the killer described in the manuscript. He had been driving a red Chevy truck with stolen plates. The description of his truck matches a statement from another witness who saw a pickup truck of that description on Sellersville Drive coming from the direction of the cabin on Wagon Trail Road on the afternoon of your daughter's disappearance."

"Can we see her?" Gillian asked.

"I can arrange that right away. Abby's body is fairly decomposed. You may want to consider cremation," Silverwood said, with an appearance of calm.

"I'll take a couple of days off from work, so the two of us can be there on Monday," Lance replied.

"I'll give you some time to settle into your hotel. So, let's say Tuesday, morning. Here's my card. I wrote the address and telephone number to the medical examiner's office in Stroudsburg on the back. Call me from the hotel you're staying if you need directions," the detective said, handing him a business card.

"Detective Silverwood, do you think you can find the man who killed my daughter?" Lance asked, a hint of emotion in his voice.

"That's what I'm trying to do."

"She didn't deserve to be killed like that," Gillian added with a shudder.

"No child does," the detective firmly replied.

Silverwood stayed with them for another hour, trying to console them. He knew no matter how badly they felt, at least they would have closure, the chance to properly mourn their daughter.

At about the same time, this news was brought to the Wincoff's in Watchung, New Jersey, serial killer Joey Marks was in the Adirondacks on a Christmas vacation. At some elongated motel, up near Tupper Lake in Franklin County, New York, he collected his room key from the reception desk. In recent months, his face had become noticeably shadowed with beard stubble.

The sight of an eleven year old girl sitting on one of the couches in the lobby caught his attention. Her parents were too busy talking to notice him standing there at the end of the aisle.

For a few brief seconds his eyes glittered with evil as he concentrated on her. Lewd thoughts echoed in his mind as he looked at her for a long, slow moment. She seemed to be his type, his only type.

In the most peculiar way, the girl caught his glance fixed on her. He half-smiled at her before he turned to go to his room.

As he moseyed down the aisle toward the rooms, he whistled softly through his teeth. Before he disappeared around the corner, he glanced over his shoulder in her direction. With a final look at the girl, he filed the image of her face in the depths of his memory.

ABOUT THE AUTHOR

ANN GREYSON is the author of the novels *Gotham Kitty*, a Recommended Read in the 2022 Author Shout Reader Ready Awards and a Silver Book Award winner in the 2021 Literary Titan Awards; *The Lonely Vampire,* a Recommended Read in the 2021 Author Shout Reader Ready Awards and First Place Paranormal in the 2021 Speak Up Talk Radio Firebird Book Awards; and *Never-DEAD,* a Finalist in Books for Teenagers in the 2021 Wishing Shelf Book Awards and a Third Place General Fiction in the 2020 TCK Publishing Reader's Choice Awards. Other writing credits include book reviews for the *Amazon* and *Goodreads* websites.

She has a passion for creating fictional characters for television, acting in the programs: *i Citizen, SpaceWoman Light-years Apart, The Lonely* Vampire, The *Out World, puRR,* and *Never-DEAD.* Ann portrays the astral projection ghostwriter Gail Wincoff in the *Birdwatcher* short television program broadcast on Manhattan Neighborhood Network's Lifestyle Channel 2 in 2019. She is the producer of *Pompilia* broadcast on Anne Arundel Community Television; *The Watchers*, a nominee for a VOLLIE Award for Best Local Documentary, and *Gotham Kitty,* a nominee for a VOLLIE Award for Best Arts/Entertainment Program, from Community Media Center TV of Westminster in 2014.

With many dancing credits on stage, she also sings and acts in the music videos: *Shine*, *O Christmas Tree*, *House of the Rising Sun*, *Motherless Child,* and *Buffalo Gals*.

Ann Greyson has an Associate of Arts degree in English from Howard Community College. She is a member of Actors' Equity Association, SAG-AFTRA and the Alpha Alpha Sigma chapter of Phi Theta Kappa. She has the honor of receiving the Albert Nelson Marquis Lifetime Achievement Award from Marquis Who's Who in 2017.

ACKNOWLEDGMENTS

The author wishes to thank Vivian Davis, Tutoring Art; and Meaghan D'Otazzo for their help in making this work of fiction ring true.